Coyote Wind

COYOTE
WIND

⚜

A GABRIEL DU PRÉ MYSTERY

Peter Bowen

St. Martin's Press
New York

Mystery
Bowen

Design by Sara Stemen

LIBRARY OF CONGRESS CATALOGING IN PUBLICATION DATA

Bowen, Peter,
    Coyote wind/Peter Bowen.
       p.   cm.
    ISBN 0-312-10957-1
    1. Sheriffs—Montana—Fiction. I. Title.
PS3552.0866C69   1994
813'.54—dc20   94–798

First Edition: July 1994

10 9 8 7 6 5 4 3 2 1

For Nancy Stringfellow

✤ CHAPTER 1 ✤

Du Pré stirred in his sleep. His eyes fluttered, opened, he looked up at the ceiling. He squinted, raised his head, glanced toward the rising light in the east, out the window of Madelaine's bedroom. Little spikes of frost reached out from the corners of the wavy old glass.

A pebble rattled against the window.

Du Pré decided it was not a dream. He slipped from the bed, a warm breath of air thick with the scent of their bodies rose from the bed. Madelaine's lips bubbled softly, it was as close as she came to snoring.

Du Pré looked out toward the street, saw a crooked shadow on the short white picket fence. White hair askelter as a forkful of hay. Old Benetsee, the fool, the drunken old breed, a singer, once a dancer, old enough to have been most anything outside of town.

"Shit," Du Pré whispered, annoyed at coming out of warm sleep for this. It passed. The old man always had a reason for bothering Du Pré, even if it sometimes took Du Pré years to see it. Benetsee. Du Pré could see him long, long ago, dancing in the deserts, his head one day smiling from a platter at while the king's wife swirled in silks and scents. God damn. Loony prophets anyway.

"Du Pré!" Madelaine, now up on an elbow, rubbing her eyes.

"Benetsee," whispered Du Pré. "I must go out, see what he wants."

1

"Take him a glass of wine," said Madelaine. "Don't tease him."

Du Pré shrugged into his clothes, pulled on his boots, one leather mule-ear pull came off with a final chuckling rip. His heel slid down. He walked to the stairs and placed his feet carefully going down, the resinous yellow pine steps creaked five times before his boot touched the worn woolen carpet at the bottom. He went to the kitchen, took a jug of cheap white wine from the icebox, poured a big glassful, lit a cigarette, went outside.

The old man was shivering, leaned up against the Russian olive tree, his bright old eyes brilliant black in his brown creased face.

Benetsee nodded, took the wine and gulped it down.

Du Pré waited, respecting the old man. He had been a good friend of Du Pré's grandparents, long dead now. Plastic flowers on their graves, dust ricking in the petals. Du Pré washed them with holy water on saints' days that had been dear to them.

"I dreamed of a coyote last night," said Benetsee, "he went up a draw, sat and howled by some people's bones."

Du Pré nodded. Benetsee's damn riddles. He wished the old fart would come to the point, which was probably five dollars. So I just give him the five dollars and go back to bed? No, the old man was not just a pest.

"Then you come and sat down on your heels and looked and looked," the old man went on, in his slurred Coyote French, "but you never saw till the coyote come back and scratch the earth."

Now my days got skeletons in them, thought Du Pré, but if the old man go to the police they throw him in jail for drunk. Me, I look at burn marks on cow asses for part of my living. It's cold out here.

Benetsee cleared his throat, waved the empty glass, looked at Du Pré hopefully.

"You have another drink you go to sleep," said Du Pré.

"Madelaine don't mind," said Benetsee. "She's a saint, you could learn from her."

Du Pré snorted, shook his head, went back in the house and got the old man another belt. Someday I find him dead in the frozen mud where he pissed his pants and passed out and stuck there, but for now, he's happy. He heard Madelaine on the stairs, she came into the kitchen, her wool robe clutched tight around her against the cold.

"He can sleep in the shed," Madelaine said. "You take him the old sleeping bag in the hall there. Also tell him good morning and when he wakes up I will make him eat something."

Du Pré smiled. Madelaine, she would feed all the earth, soothe its pains and hungers. She was as simple and straightforward and generous as the sunlight.

And she knows what's bothering me before I do, Du Pré thought. He smiled at his luck.

Du Pré opened the door and pushed the storm door away with his foot, scooped up the sleeping bag. A slop of wine drooled down his hand, he smelled the alcohol.

The old man sniffed the wine happily, drank it in a single long draught.

"Madelaine says you got to eat, you wake up," said Du Pré.

"I do what Madelaine say," said Benetsee, taking the sleeping bag and walking off toward the shed. There was an old army cot in it, on the duckboards. Flowerpots and bags of fertilizer, garden tools on nails, sanctuary.

Du Pré watched him go, smiled, went back in the house.

❧ CHAPTER 2 ❧

Du Pré signed off on the two truckloads of steers. The brands were good and the destinations usual. Feedlots in Nebraska, then to pot roasts in Chicago or St. Louis. The drivers pulled away, the long double-deck trailers stinking, green shit running down here and there from airholes, ammonia and bawling. The buyer's check had been handed over to the Oleson brothers, Ike and Earl, in their sixties now and bent as any other old cowboys, a life of fractures and strange strains of work which bowed the bones and made the hands grow huge. They knew horses, wore farmer shoes and tractor-driver hats, claimed it was so that folks wouldn't think they were just truck drivers.

"Some fine day," said Ike, wiping sweat from his forehead with a hand gnarled as old roots. "Earl busted his ankle again chowsing them cows outa the brush. I was too old for this forty years ago, thought I'd maybe do something else, but here I gone and done it anyway."

Du Pré chuckled. What was this place, Montana? Breeds, and squareheads from Scandahoovia, other families from the common American ruck. The land was tough and poor and so were the people. Old cars and old shacks fell into the earth, people starved out in the twenties, left the dried-out dust-eaten little ranches with their homes in their hands. Too poor then to buy grease for the axles of their wagons. The wooden wagon beds could be found beside hundreds of the little trails, gone silver from the sun, parts of them charred from the wheels catching fire where they rubbed the axles to flame.

"When you going to fiddle again?" Du Pré said, looking at Ike Oleson. The old cowboy, never married, a Hardänger fiddler, two extra drone strings on his sawbox. Du Pré fiddled, too, but just the old four-string kind, like his ancestors, the voyageurs, with their red sashes and little tobacco pipes, tasseled caps and the beaded moccasins.

"Sunday afternoon," said Oleson, "at the bar in Toussaint. Good Swede music, then we let you play to clear the hall."

Du Pré heard the *squak squak squak* of his two-way radio, the dispatcher's stripped voice. What's this? Well, sometimes I get to play lawman, when the Sheriff's deputies are all tangled up. I even have a gun somewhere in that car, I think the trunk. Maybe under the front seat.

Du Pré walked to his old Plymouth, actually bought from the cops, shorn of lights and siren, but still with clips on the door for a rifle and one small bullet hole in the rear window.

"Du Pré," he said, pressing down the red button on the mike.

"Gabe!" boomed the Sheriff's voice, big loud man, everyone liked him even though he sometimes hurt their ears.

"Yes."

"We got a bad wreck on the highway near the Res—and Toomey is off with that busted arm. Them rich drunks own that big house in the foothills of the Wolf Mountains, you know the place?"

"Yah," said Du Pré. Everyone knew the place, ten thousand square feet of house, bigger than the high school in Pomeroy, for Chrissakes, looked like it dropped from space. The people in it came from East Coast money, lots of it, enough to hire help for everything.

"One of their hands claims he found a plane wreck and some skeletons or something up in a dry draw, up high, he was looking around, he said. Probably chasing a deer he shouldn't have shot. Wonder if you'd go look?"

"Don't the FAA handle that?"

"I called them," said the Sheriff. "They got no record of any missing plane could be where the cowboy says it is, so they want proof it is one 'fore they get off their asses."

"Can I get a horse there?" said Du Pré.

"Talk to this guy found it, name's Bodie, I'd think so."

"Am I gettin' paid for this," Du Pré wondered loudly, knowing the answer.

"You know we ain't got that kind of money," said the Sheriff.

"For my gas, at least?"

"Yeah, yeah." Bullshit bullshit.

Du Pré wondered if the cowboy had got kicked in the head or something, was seeing things, like Benetsee.

"OK, I'll do it," said Du Pré. "You call Madelaine, tell her I be late, hear?"

"SURE!" boomed the Sheriff. Du Pré winced.

"What's that all about?" said Ike Oleson.

"I dunno," said Du Pré, "some shit about a plane crash in the mountains. I got to go look at it."

"Up past them rich shits, in the Wolfs?"

Du Pré nodded.

"Hell," Ike said, "I bet them people see things like that all the time. I saw Mrs. Fascelli out there once, she sashayed buck naked across the lawn wavin' an umbrella, singin' she was Mary Poppins or some damn thing."

"No shit," said Du Pré. "Well, they drink a lot, I guess."

"Glad I don't have money," said Oleson.

Du Pré nodded, and got into his car.

✤ CHAPTER 3 ✤

You don't look like no cop," said the young cowboy, Bodie. He looked very stupid. Ragged dirty shirt, stained old wool vest, brand-new jeans with the price tags still on them.

"Auxiliary," said Du Pré.

"What's that?" said Bodie, his little eyes narrowing. Too many syllables, Du Pré was making fun of him.

"Part-time," said Du Pré.

Bodie considered the hyphenate, spat in the dust.

"I need a horse," said Du Pré, "and you guide me up where you found this wreck." You stupid son of a bitch.

"You think I'm lyin'?" hissed Bodie. "It's a plane, propeller and everything, lotta bones, couple skulls."

"No, I don't think you lyin'," said Du Pré. I think you're so fucking dumb you probably found an old campfire and two white rocks or something. And I pick out the horse I want, they must all hate you a lot.

"Hey!" A shout from the huge stone and glass and redwood house, a fat red face hanging out a window.

"Who the fuck are you?" said the face. Someone inside pulled, the face disappeared.

"Don't mind him," said Bodie. "He's about ready to go off to the dry-out place again."

Bodie walked away, Du Pré followed. He had stopped at a little grocery and beer place on the way, bought jerky and candy bars and a couple butane lighters, case he had to stay out overnight. Late as it was, he would.

Bodie threw Du Pré a catch-rope, pointed to a small cavvy of horses, began hauling saddles, blankets, and tack out of the shed. Clouds were stacking up over the wolf country, high, stuck on the peaks. Du Pré saw an eagle floating motionless. Good. Never mind he had to hold the road map out as far as his arms could stretch to make out the names of the larger towns. Glasses had a way of getting lost and broken.

The trail went straight up through a big fenced pasture, overgrazed, though the fences were so new and well done they could only belong to an owner who needed more to lose money than to make money in the cow business. Bodie rode ahead, fighting a little with the movements of his horse. One of those lousy riders who will never get any better. The horse kept swinging his head side to side, obviously pissed off.

Du Pré looked up at the island mountain range, the nine peaks, robed round with bluffs and foothills. They rose up strangely from the high dry plains, catching enough water from the eastering clouds to make them green with trees and shrubs. The sight of them against the northern sky was as familiar to Du Pré as the house he was raised in and lived in still. Strangers to the country remarked on their beauty. Du Pré was uncomfortable in lands that didn't look like this. It simply was meant to look like this. Home.

Bodie's horse shied, a rattlesnake had sunned upon a flat warm spot on the trail. The bad young cowboy flew hot in rage, beat on the horse until the animal reared and fell over on its side. Du Pré thought he heard Bodie's leg snap. He hoped he had.

"Goddamn it to fucking hell," the boy screamed, hands clasped to thigh.

Du Pré swung down, dropped the reins. His horse stood there, knew Du Pré's hand, knew him. Bodie's horse trotted away, once stepping on a rein and jerking his head. Du Pré knelt by the cowboy, felt the leg. Not broken, but the muscles torn and swelling.

"I'll shoot that fucking horse!" Bodie snarled through his pain.

"No you won't," said Du Pré. "You're not bad hurt. Now, I go catch him for you and you ride on back and you be good to that damn horse. I get back and see his mouth's torn or you hurt him, then I kick your stupid teeth down your throat."

The cowboy gaped at Du Pré.

"It ain't broken?" he said.

Du Pré spat, walked back to his horse. He swung up, went off after Bodie's rangy gelding. Idiot. Shoveling life's shit with a broken handle.

The pony stood waiting, looking back at Du Pré. He grabbed the reins and led him back.

"He'll take you," said Du Pré. "Now where you find this wreck?"

"Little dry draw third shoulder over," said Bodie.

"You just let that horse carry you back," said Du Pré. "I hope he dumps you and kicks you to death. He does, I buy him, feed him oats and carrots every day, molasses. You're too stupid to live."

"My leg . . ." Bodie whimpered.

"Fuck your leg," said Du Pré. He rode on. Before the trail turned he looked back. The cowboy was struggling to mount, the horse's ears were back.

More in the world like him than not, Du Pré thought. God damn it, be like that. Shit.

✤ CHAPTER 4 ✤

He found it right where Bodie had said it was. A mess, yes, but a very old one. A juniper had grown up through the metal frame of a seat. Rusted engine half-buried in the yellow earth of the draw. Bones were scattered around, the coyotes and skunks and badgers would have come along and supped. When this had happened the draw had burned, maybe it had been a rainy night, but it had been a long time ago. The plane had been a light, flimsy one, the marks it would have made when it hit so long ago had been erased.

Du Pré stamped his feet. It was cold, maybe ten above. He had spent the night crouched over a little fire, a saddle blanket on his shoulders.

Candy bars and stale water for breakfast. Madelaine was in bed. Missing him. He hoped.

The light rose. Du Pré cast around, quartered back and forth. He looked down at the place where the sagebrush trunk went into the ground. A jawbone, human. The skull then rolls downhill. So he walked straight down, like water would run. The draw was pretty steep, not much water had moved through it.

The skull was nestled under a flat rock which crossed the little streambed. The spring melts were running through the gravels underneath the slab. Lucky the skull was still whole.

Du Pré knelt, looked, crossed himself. Some days he

didn't believe in God, but he did believe in crossing himself.

"Maybe this let you sleep now," said Du Pré. He picked up the white skull, the color of the giant puffball mushrooms that came up in pastures in the wet years. The mushrooms were bigger, and startling in the green.

"Now I got someone's head in my hands, I thinking on frying mushrooms," Du Pré said aloud. "Dumb bastard."

Du Pré turned the skull in his hands. A neat hole in the forehead of it. Something rattled inside. A thin bone at the back, near where the spine joined, had been chewed through by a coyote, so the brains could be licked out. A slug fell out of the hole, landed on a bed of broken lime between stones. Dull gray, dull green. Copper jacket then. Du Pré stared at it.

He looked again at the hole in the skull, punched when the bone was living, dished, like an awl hole through tin.

Du Pré put the slug in his pocket, snapped the flap shut. He looked up toward the place where the rusting engine stained the earth. The sun was up enough now to begin making clouds, little misty wisps, from the flanks of the mountains where the frost had bloomed the night before. They would gather above the peaks, be thick by afternoon.

He put the skull and jawbone in a saddlebag, picked again over the ground, found another jawbone. Older, drier, the teeth had slipped from the sockets. If there had been teeth in them. Well.

Du Pré stood up, arched his back, still cramped from the night's cold.

"Enough," he said. More than. Now the FAA cops would come and sift carefully for all the remnants. Haul the engine down the mountains. Ask tough questions of the hawks and coyotes? A lot of years ago.

The case would get filed and jawed over in the saloons,

but nothing more, no plane supposed to be here at all. File and forget. A bullet hole in the skull.

Du Pré picked his way back down the draw, leading the horse. The pony was gentle as a puppy, unwilling to give trouble where none was offered, like most creatures. Damn that fool Bodie anyway, he give a bad name to men.

I just don't think they ever find out on this one, not ever. Du Pré whispered a novena, looked back at the place of death. Well, every place was that for something. Du Pré stepped on a spider.

The horse knew the way home, snuffled a little. The sounds of his hooves picked up tempo as the grade flattened. Maybe he thought Bodie had been replaced by Du Pré, now the opportunities for goldbricking would be greater and the new rider wouldn't rip his mouth up with a bad hand on the reins.

Du Pré stopped for water at a little spring purling out of a red band of stone, wreathed in watercress shiny with little black beetles. He plucked a few leaves, shook off most of the bugs. Chewed. The bitter crispness freshened his mouth, the sour taste of old candy bars left.

By sunset he was at the Sheriff's office, the Sheriff chewing mints to mask the Saturday whiskey he allowed himself in adult portions. Let others arrest the amateur drunks, I run this outfit. Nobody should be Sheriff who wants the job.

"Fuck," said the Sheriff, looking at the skull, the hole in it, the jawbones, the slug Du Pré dropped on the counter for punctuation. "Now them FAA's got to come." He turned the slug around in his fingers. "How come you didn't put this in an evidence bag?"

"Didn't have any," said Du Pré. "Remember, I inspect brands. They don't make evidence bags big enough put a cow in."

The Sheriff looked at him hard, fuzzed up, trying to come back but too much Canadian hooch on his tongue, just sitting there.

"What about that cowboy found this?"

"Oh, no," said Du Pré. "That dummy, he wasn't even born this happened. No. Anyway, he's too stupid to do any killing, 'cept maybe his mother or girl when he's drunk. He'll end up in Deer Lodge, he's dumber than a box of rocks."

"What do you think of this?" said the Sheriff. He was staring up at the ceiling, trying to get sober.

"I don't," said Du Pré. "I don't understand it. I'm glad I don't have to."

Du Pré dusted his hands, picked up his hat.

"Where you goin'?"

"Confession," said Du Pré. "I go to Mass in the morning."

"Well, good luck."

Du Pré's eyes crinkled. He laughed.

✤ CHAPTER 5 ✤

I'm still living in sin with Madelaine Placquemines," said Du Pré, to the dim shadow behind the confessional screen.

"Good," said Father Van Den Heuvel.

"Also I wanted to kill somebody." Du Pré thought of shooting Bodie. It made him happy. Bodie bled in the dust and the horses smiled at Du Pré.

"Did you?"

"No," said Du Pré. Good idea, though.

"Two sins. Good week. Got any more, I'm running a special."

"Don't think so."

"Couple Hail Marys. The words are pretty, you'll like them."

The priest absolved him.

Du Pré struggled out of the booth, looked at the few others who were waiting. His daughter Jacqueline, pregnant again, flowing.

Du Pré the grandfather, at forty. Five times over. She started young with her man. Fifteen, him seventeen. She wanted twelve. Du Pré didn't want to remember that many names, but he supposed he could.

He stopped and bent over to kiss her. She smelled beautiful, no perfume, just her.

"You come by, eat?" Jacqueline murmured.

"Sure," said Du Pré, "what we bring?"

"Wine and your fiddle."

Du Pré walked out of the church, smiling. His wife died so suddenly, cancer of the blood, seemed like a bad cold till she died just like that, less than two weeks. The two girls, four and nine then, very bad time. Jacqueline got very mad personally with Death, take one of hers she send back twelve till Death give up. Just you wait and see, for sure.

And my other daughter, child of the times, Du Pré thought, grimacing. Horrible, loud, mean music, forty lipsticks all at once, the only roached hair in the town.

Poor Du Pré, the mothers of the families said, while their children got drunk and knocked each other up or finally got through school and went off to the service or college or, often enough, to Deer Lodge Prison when the judge's patience ran clean out.

He wondered for a moment if Maria was still a virgin. Probably not. All things taken into account, probably none of Du Pré's business. She was a young woman of fourteen, going on twenty-five. When she got to twenty-five, she'd look back and wince. Like everybody.

I don't know the proper noises to make, Du Pré thought. I could threaten her with convent boarding school. She'd laugh. She keeps trying to piss me off. I think. If I get mad, she cries. I do not understand any of my women.

He drove out of the town toward his house. Maria's boyfriend's old pickup truck was in the driveway and loud horrible noises came from the house. Some people might think it was music, but Du Pré knew better.

Du Pré parked his car, went on in. The two had been necking on the couch or whatever, Du Pré had enough sense to flick his headlights coming up the drive and smoke a cigarette before coming in. When you just walk on in like a dumbass you deserve what you get, anyway.

The living room smelled of beer. Lust. People.

Maria and her boyfriend—what was his name, Raymond? Dark and surly kid with high-top running shoes, embarrassed at not knowing what the fuck was going on anywhere, like any other boy his age.

"TURN THAT SHIT OFF!" Du Pré roared. His head hurt. Maria, pouting a bit for appearance's sake, punched the button on the record player, and it died.

For this, no resurrection, Du Pré thought. Hah.

"Good evening, Raymond," said Du Pré to the boy.

"He's Billy," said Maria, eyes narrowing, "and he's been Billy for some time."

Du Pré nodded.

"Sorry," he said. I'm not, either.

Billy looked at the floor and his untied shoelaces.

"You got a report card?" said Du Pré. I play father, maybe she be nice and not laugh at me in front of Billy, here.

Maria brought it. She got very good grades, though Du Pré had never seen a textbook in the house. Just magazines.

"Very good, daughter," said Du Pré. "All A's, one B, who was this prick anyway? She didn't get this from *me*.

Maria smiled, they would hug later.

If she needs me to take care of her some way I'll do it, thought Du Pré, but I am afraid to try it on my own. He looked at Billy. Was I as dumb, clumsy, and loutish as this boy? Undoubtedly. It's a wonder there are any people at all, something didn't eat us all a million years ago. I see Billy, I cannot believe in evolution. It is not a religious matter.

Don't make fun of the boy, it hurts forever.

"We go to dinner at your sister's tomorrow?" said Du Pré.

"No, I got something else," said Maria. She didn't like her sister these days, having beautiful babies, being a real woman, damn age anyway.

Du Pré thought Maria would shoot out of this place like a missile, get an education, and what Du Pré thought of that no matter. He thought it was wonderful, but didn't want to screw anything up by approving at the wrong time.

I don't know how to do this, Du Pré thought, Jackie and Maria do. I think. I hope.

"I'll be at Madelaine's," said Du Pré.

Like I always am, and all the kids will be drinking beer here and maybe smoking a little grass, but I have never come back at a reasonable hour of the morning to find the place not cleaned up, so I suppose she is not trying to tell me anything.

I don't understand any of my women and I am not going to, it is beyond me and that's that.

He walked down the gravel walk, looked out at the horse pasture and his six head, standing there in a circle, plotting something.

"Just keep quiet, Daddy Du Pré," he said to himself, "An' let your daughters take care of you, or if you don't, make noises, they will *really* take care of you."

Know that for sure, yes I do.

♣ CHAPTER 6 ♣

Du Pré was prepared for complete assholes, these FAA's. But they turned out to be pleasant weary professionals who sorted out death and destruction, maybe save someone's life down the road. Unlike the FBI and BATF agents, who were jerks to begin with and then exiled to Montana to boot. Made them vicious. Take Leonard Peltier, for instance, take Wounded Knee. The second one.

Their work made the FAA inspectors direct.

"You Indian?" one said. Not "Native American."

"Some," said Du Pré. "A lot, really. But Frenchy enough so the anthropologists don't bother us."

"A blessing," said the FAA man. "My sister was married to an anthropologist for a while."

The FAA men had come in by plane and a helicopter had been chartered from a local cropduster. Du Pré hated helicopters. The fucking things could not possibly fly, or anyway not long enough. *Whack whack whack.* I ask you.

Du Pré sat by the pilot to point out the way.

The flight was short, a few minutes. A horse gives you time to get there, Du Pré thought. The noisy shaking machine touched down on a barren flat spot less than half a mile from the crash. The FAA agents, just two of the four, the others would come the next trip, got out with their cases of cameras and metal detectors.

Du Pré had helped sort through one other crash, but it was fresh and stinking. This was very old, here. The only smell was pine and sage.

Du Pré helped carry the equipment, his load a tripod and a heavy backpack full of something or other.

He led them up, the older agent wheezed a little.

Du Pré stopped by the rusting half-buried engine. The two FAA men looked around, whistling.

"Long time ago," said the older man. He'd got his breath back.

"Beats intestines hanging from the trees," said the other one. With such a job black humor let you sleep at night, among other things.

"I suppose I stay out of the way?" said Du Pré.

"Oh, no," said the older one. "Mr. Du Pré, we're city folks. If you could look around, maybe spot something. You'd be better than us at seeing things that were out of place."

Du Pré nodded, rolled a cigarette and smoked, watching them set up their cameras and take out tape measures and a box of plastic bags. For parts of planes. Parts of people. Long time ago.

Du Pré looked up the draw, up at a weathered cliff, the common gray stone of these mountains. There was a yellow scar of fresh rock thirty feet from the top. He won-

18

dered if the plane had hit there. Bounced back. Wait, an old Ponderosa pine rotting into the ground, laid out like a pointer from the scar on the rock to the engine buried in the yellow earth. A spray of rotted branches clustered round the little block of steel. The trunk of the tree was slumping into dust, spilling red sawdust from the jaws of the big black carpenter ants.

"Hey," said Du Pré, "I think maybe it hit up there, then land in the crown of the tree. Maybe the tree was already dead, they get hit by lightning. Then it went over, roots rotted out."

". . . And then the engine and such landed here when the tree come down. Maybe. Maybe I'm full of shit, too."

"I like this guy," said the younger FAA man. "Sounds good, even the full of shit part."

"Can we get up there?" said the older man, pointing at the scar on the cliff wall.

Du Pré looked. "Need a rope, you can't climb this rock, it's too rotten. But anything hit there, it should fall to that ledge below, should still be there. I can get to that, easy enough."

"If you find Judge Crater or Nixon's integrity or anything, you call down, we'll bag it up."

Du Pré climbed up slowly through the rubbled rock the ledge had shed to frost. When he finally rolled up on to the flat he sat up and saw an easier way, good game path on it, fifty feet away. Always worked out like that, life.

The grass and shrubs were sparse, spalled scree littered the ledge. Good place for rattlesnakes. He quartered back and forth, saw a square black corner, tugged a radio from the duff, beneath it was a gauge of some kind with the glass broken out.

"I found a radio and a gauge," Du Pré called down. "You want to come up or I just bring it to you?"

"God damn it, look again, and don't see anything," the younger man laughed. He picked up some plastic bags, slung his camera and bag on his shoulder. He started up the way Du Pré had gone.

"It's easier over there," Du Pré called down, pointing to his right.

Du Pré looked down at his boot. There was a coyote turd there, a rope of deer hair from a scavenged kill, and the gleaming tiny skull of a shrew.

Du Pré put the scat in his pocket, snapped the flap.

❦ CHAPTER 7 ❦

How nice you come see me now and again," said Madelaine. "I already have one husband run off, now my boyfriend is practicing, yes? Hunh?"

Du Pré grinned at her. His wife dead, her husband gone crazy, maybe even dead, gone three years, not a peep. She wanted to divorce him for desertion but the Church says wait. I want to marry this woman but God won't let me. Bullshit.

Father Van Den Heuvel says about the same thing. No wonder he's here, ass end of nowhere, him a very educated man. Among the heathen I should wear my red sash more.

"I marry you today, Madelaine," said Du Pré. "Go and roust the Judge."

"I don't care what the Judge think," said Madelaine. "I care what God may think."

A good girl, four children, not wanting to blow Paradise.

God, He ought to get to work on time, stay later, tend to business.

All four of her kids were doing good in the schools, happy kids, poor, lots of love here and Madelaine firm on doing one's best. And working in the huge garden out back, where the stuffs they canned for the winter grew. When you sweat to grow what you eat it fills you up better.

"So what's this airplane's name? Uh. Debbie?"

"Bonnie," said Du Pré. An old and loving game they played.

"Well," said Madelaine, letting her robe fall open, "I 'spose I love that you still have some time for me, you bastard."

They went to bed, hot flesh, need, lay spent.

"I got to go out northwest for a while," said Du Pré. "I got a feeling someone is maybe selling beef too quick."

"Who?" said Madelaine.

"Oh," said Du Pré, "I don't know, be a brand inspector, you just got to show up a lot of places where you not supposed to be at all. You know, kill a beef and sell it out of your car to people. Or back up a small truck with a portable chute, load it quick and take the cattle to a small slaughterhouse, the owner pays in cash, good deal for everyone but the poor rancher."

"Now I got to worry, a cow," said Madelaine. "What's her name?"

"Josephine."

"I got a daughter named Josephine . . ."

"She's six, too old for me," said Du Pré.

"Beast."

Du Pré got up, dressed.

"Du Pré," said Madelaine, "that daughter you got, she

21

could come live here, you know. I make her put her hair back nice."

"Oh," said Du Pré.

"Oh. What. Oh? She shames you running around like that with that worthless stupid Billy."

"I'm not shamed by her," said Du Pré. "Thing about Maria is she's her own. They both are."

"That damn hair."

"Madelaine," said Du Pré, patiently, "I know that you want to help. Well, help me. You try to run Maria, she'll buck. She's a good girl, she just doen't want to be a breed girl in bunghole Montana. She'll go away, find that there are worse things to be, try some of them. My daughters take good care of me."

"How's that?"

"They don't tell me everything," said Du Pré.

"Women don't never tell everything," said Madelaine. She grinned.

"Josephine, I'm coming," Du Pré sang. He had a good tenor, good for the chansons, good for the reels. Sometimes when he sang he felt his people back there a couple centuries, little French-Cree-Chippewa *voyageurs*, singing while they hauled the heavy packs of furs to Sault Sainte Marie for the Company of Gentlemen Adventurers of Hudson Bay. The HBC. Here Before Christ, to some.

They sweated and starved and froze, those little *voyageurs*. The men who made the money off the furs died of gout and port.

"Say," said Madelaine, "I want to hear you fiddle some this time soon—I see there is a fiddler's jamboree on Saturday. Maybe I even let you drink too much wine."

"Sure," said Du Pré.

"If Josephine let you go," said Madelaine, pouting.

"I ask her," said Du Pré.

Madelaine threw a shoe at him.

✤ C H A P T E R   8 ✤

The big old saloon was crowded, it had been built back in the days when ranchers had lots of hands instead of lots of machinery. A lot of fiddlers here, even some college boys from somewhere, all trying to make authentic music. They didn't seem to know what music was, but they were hell-bent on authentic.

Du Pré set his violin case down on a small table, helped Madelaine with her coat.

"Josephine says I can stay late, drink a lot, stop off and see her on the way home," said Du Pré.

"Moo," said Madelaine. "I want some wine."

Pink wine. Sweet. Kind she liked was made out of bubble gum, Du Pré thought.

Du Pré got her a big glass, himself some whiskey. The woman behind the bar had a lacquered beehive hairdo, blond and white, with dark roots. Her hands were red from washing everything.

The Oleson brothers came in, dressed alike, new denims and the railroad red cotton kerchief. Ike was carrying the mangy case his curly-maple Hardänger fiddle slept in.

Du Pré hated Hardänger music. He claimed it had been invented to scare herring into the nets. *Scree. Scraw.* But he liked Ike Oleson.

The college boys were murdering "The Red-Haired Boy," a tune Du Pré would like to have heard in other than a tortured state. While the boys screeked away, they stared at Du Pré and the Olesons. Jesus Christ, Justin, there's some real ones. Right, Nigel.

"You look good there," said Ike, coming by, taking his hat off to Madelaine. Elderly bachelor, always a gentleman to the ladies, who scared him witless.

"You lookin' good, Dupree," said Oleson. Du Pré wondered what chickenshit television program the old fart had been watching. Du Pré indeed. These English, even if they were Swede.

"You play that Injun fiddle, eh?" said a big half-drunk man, so drunk it seemed a reasonable question to him.

"Wahoo," said Du Pré, turning away. The man went off.

"Play 'The Steep Portage,' Du Pré," said Madelaine.

"I want to wait a minute," said Du Pré, "see them tune." There were a dozen fiddlers twisting keys, the college boys would be tuned by the century's end.

Du Pré looked down at his feet, beaded moccasins in red and turquoise and yellow and black. Old Nez Percé woman over in Idaho did them. Du Pré had asked her if they were old Nez Percé designs. She had said no, she got them out of a book in a language she could not read.

"What language?" Du Pré asked.

"Japanese!" said the old woman, laughing.

"Hey! Du Pré!" Buster Lacroix from fifty miles east, played the rib bones.

Du Pré fiddled, Buster thocked out the rhythm hard. He made the good ringing bones from the third rib of a fat steer, aged them in the shitpile, or so he said.

The college boys looked hungrily at the two of them. Go

24

be some professors, Du Pré thought, we got to work our lives.

Some of the Métis women began to dance, the old reels and Cree glories, leftovers from the days when the Red River carts with their huge cottonwood wheels skreeked and scrawked down from the north to hunt the buffalo. The Métis drove the buffalo into stout blind corrals or drove the herds from swift surefooted buffalo ponies. Make everybody meat for the winter. The carts sounded for many miles over the prairies. At night the men gambled. The leaders were all poor, like those of the Indians who were the lost generous and humble. Wealth was a sign of a bad heart. The more power you had, the less you owned. Nobody who ever wanted a chief's job got it.

Take that, you white fools who want to be president.

Madelaine got up, joined the ring of dancing women. Her heavy breasts swung while she danced. She threw back her head, laughed, her white even teeth startling in her brown face. Her black hair flashed crimson, sheen of fire.

Long ago the English hanged poor mad Louis Riel, him with his visions and little talks with God, Jesus, the Holy Ghost, the saints Louis had heard of. Many of the Métis came down to Montana. To the old buffalo grounds, just before the buffalo were all slaughtered, just before the great cattle drives began. North to fatten scrawny Texas steers on good Montana grass, Texans came with the cattle, and Montanans hated them then and hate them still.

Gabriel danced too much and fiddled too much and drank too much. Madelaine danced too much and drank too much sweet pink wine and she flirted with the men, who laughed and nudged each other.

When they left, the fiddles were wobbling in search of the right notes.

25

Gabriel was too drunk to go to confession, so was Madelaine.

In the night the telephone rang. It was the Sheriff's office. Maria and some other kids had been busted, beer, a little dope. The Sheriff would let her go if Du Pré came to get her.

"No," said Gabriel, "I leave her there till morning."

Madelaine was half-asleep, but she woke up for that.

"You won't go get your own daughter out of jail?" she said.

"It would just make her mad with me if I did," said Du Pré. "See, that girl likes taking her licks for her own doings, you know? They are both pretty tough, my girls."

"I don't know," said Madelaine.

"My girls, I do," said Du Pré.

He went and fetched Maria early in the morning. They said nothing to one another while he drove her home.

She kissed him on the cheek and said a soft "thank you."

That be that, thought Du Pré. Whew.

✦ CHAPTER 9 ✦

Du Pré came back from checking out a long stretch of fence that was seldom watched. Ranchers were so pressed for time that often they did not miss stolen stock until the fall roundup, if the thieves repaired the fence. Du Pré watched for tire tracks in the barrow pits, fences a little saggy, maybe new wire bright on a splice. You could get a couple thousand dollars in a truck in a hurry. Beat wages, yes it did.

But he hadn't seen anything. Times like this he had his gun on the seat, in its holster. He'd arrested two men a few years before, one of them actually reaching for a rifle when Du Pré had shot and winged the bastard, shattering the man's upper arm. Then the judge let the guy off easy, on account of the trouble of his arm.

"He reach that rifle, maybe I'd be dead," said Du Pré. "Damn his fuckin' arm anyway."

No one paid any attention to Du Pré. The man got a year. Suspended.

So much, thought Du Pré, for my fuckin' civil rights, like breathing.

When he had offered that opinion the judge threatened him with jail for contempt.

The world was in a sack, for sure, Du Pré thought.

Used to be, Montana, you just shot them, said to the judge that they needed killing, went to the saloon.

Du Pré looked down the road from the top of the Big Bench toward Toussaint. The yellow-gray packed dirt, ribboning down to the shabby little town. The Sheriff's big fat cruiser, more damn lights on it than a Vegas hotel, coming up toward Du Pré.

I don't like this, Du Pré thought. I am a cow-ass man. A specialist in burnt skin and hair. Pyrography, I think that they call it. Shit. He hoped the Sheriff's car would blow up or something.

Du Pré pulled over to a snowplow turnaround, big pile of sand to spread on the icy spots, little gravel in the sand so big trucks can blast holes in your windshield when they pass you. He got out, rolled a cigarette, smoked it, wished he would quit. Bad for you, but I like it.

The Sheriff's cruiser slowed, turned in, parked beside Du Pré.

"Du Pré," the big man boomed, "I got news. That plane

went down thirty-five years ago, rancher and his wife from the Dakotas, someplace, Pembina I think. Didn't file a flight plan or nothing. You know how the people are around here. Government *says* I *got* to do something, fuck them till they ask politely, then maybe I'll think about it."

Du Pré nodded. He knew what the people around here were like, sure enough. Hell, when Montana convened its first legislature the first elected governor refused to swear allegiance to the damn Yankees, claiming that Pemberton's Missouri army had just marched northwest and was still in the game. The legislature removed the offending language from the oath of office. Kill a Montanan, you got to cut off their head, bury it where they can't find it.

"There's parts of *three* people up there, though. They got most of two skeletons. And another skull and extra fingers and hand bones."

"Sonofabitch," said Du Pré. "The Headless Man."

The Sheriff nodded.

A generation ago, when Du Pré was still a boy, twelve, maybe, a rancher found a corpse without head or hands, pretty rotten, too, dumped in a culvert. Not a tooth or a fingerprint to go on. Guy had an appendix operation scar, couple other dings. No clothing. Du Pré remembered his father talking about it, the year before he died.

"Bloated up pretty good," said Du Pré's father, a brand inspector, too, quiet guy, called "Catfoot" because he never wore anything but moccasins and barely ruffled the dust when he walked.

"We haul him out, coroner let the gas out of him, man, what a stink. So we send the meat off to the state lab, they send back a paper says the guy is dead, sure enough, so we wouldn't worry, and without anything to identify him with. They ask around, see if anyone got a head and a pair of hands, want the rest of the act. But no. Guy was about thirty-five, white, and that's all anyone ever knows. Had his appendix out, but it didn't help him much, I guess."

"Long before my time," said the Sheriff, "I didn't move here from the Bighorn country till seventy-five."

"Well, maybe," said Du Pré. He wondered why the Sheriff always shouted. Maybe he was deaf, too vain to wear a hearing aid. Maybe he was just a loud bastard.

"Report's at the office," said the Sheriff. "Maybe you could look at it."

"I ain't a cop," said Du Pré.

"Yeah," shouted the Sheriff, "But your people go back more'n a century here, maybe you know somebody knows something."

Du Pré spat at a beetle struggling through the gravel under his boots.

"I mean," said the Sheriff, "you ought to be a little curious, at least."

"No more than to lean over, someone telling the whole story in a bar," said Du Pré.

Du Pré got in his car, drove off toward Toussaint, and the Sheriff's office in Cooper, few miles on.

"Why," he said to himself, "would somebody go to all that trouble, kill someone, cut off the head and hands, hump them up into the Wolf Mountains, stick them in an old plane wreck. Knew the country good, knew about the plane wreck. Knew it better than all these folks who spent their lives poking around in this country, find the Lost Bullfrog Mine or something."

Or was it something else?

Du Pré thought. He remembered spitting on a dirty rock once, and a head rose up out of the coils, and the rattle started.

But before he spat, it was just a rock, you hear?

✤ CHAPTER 10 ✤

Du Pré hadn't liked reporters since he met one. They had very bad manners and they always got everything wrong or if they got anything right they misspelled it. One had come a few years back to do a piece on the fiddlers and he spelled Métis "Metissé," like a goddamned movie writer or something.

The movie people were so much worse they were kind of fun. One bunch had hired Du Pré at two hundred a day as a "consultant" while they made some piece of crap about a Sioux kept a pet grizzly—they thought grizzlies ate soybeans or something—and every time this Sioux killed a buffalo he held a wake for it. All the Sioux's relatives keening over this fine buffalo, good fellow, strong, brave, great singer and dancer, forgive us for making stew out of you our brother. The Sioux was extreme badasses, and before the whites give them horses and guns they was eating each other and any Cree that they could catch. As in, "We feeling peckish, so it is *you*, Least Muskrat. Apologies to you for we are eating you our brother." But never mind.

The deputy got the report for Du Pré, passed it over the counter, right under the nose of some watery-eyed asshole from the *Great Falls Tribune*. The reporter very much wanted to talk to Du Pré, as Du Pré had found the wreck.

"No, I didn't," said Du Pré. "The wreck was found by a cowboy named Bodie, works for the Crossed Eyes Ranch.

Big house, looks like it belongs in a big city, up the road toward the Wolfs."

"The Crossed Eyes Ranch?" said the reporter.

Du Pré nodded.

"Oh, bullshit," said the deputy. "It's the old Higgins place, but he's right about the house. Bodie's gone, though."

"Gone?" said Du Pré.

"Yeah," said the deputy. "Seems he owed a bunch of child support and his name wasn't Bodie anyway. So he's in jail in Miles City."

"Ho," said the reporter. "So I could talk to Mr. Dew Preee?"

"He's dead," said Du Pré. The deputy pointed and rolled his eyes.

Du Pré grunted, reading the simple report. Remains of three people, two had died of impact and fire, most likely, and the one extra skull with a bullet hole in it, the slug was probably a .38, but so weathered all the striations had long since worn off.

The hole in the skull was the sort a .38 could make, or a pole barn spike, or a meteorite that size. The skull with the hole in it lasted longer because it was not all crunched up when the plane hit and probably had arrived there at a later date, maybe.

The examining pathologist signed off, probably laughing at the very thought of ever finding out any more about this particular homicide, maybe, by bullet or pole barn spike or meteorite, maybe.

"Could I see that?" said the reporter, looking at the paper in Du Pré's hand.

"Sorry," said the deputy, taking the paper. "It's a murder under investigation." (Fuck You.)

"Could I talk to you, Mr. Dew Preee?"

31

Du Pré looked at the asshole. "I'm a brand inspector," he said.

"But you found the plane."

"Yeah," said Du Pré, "but I got a bunch of cow asses I got to go kiss. I ain't a cop. I don't have anything to do with this."

Du Pré walked out, got into his car, decided to go on home, maybe see how Maria was and if she wanted to talk to him, which she probably didn't.

He hoped the reporter would go up, talk to the rich drunks, get his shoes puked on.

Du Pré turned down the side road to his house, saw a crabbed figure tacking and yawing on the right side, sometimes throwing up his arms and tossing his head back. Nearly falling over.

Benetsee. Three parts drunk out of a possible two. Headed for Du Pré's house. First time, since Benetsee used to come by, see the Catfoot, the two of them would go and pick arrowheads out of the plowed fields in the spring, pull mussel shells out of the creeks for their wives to make buttons from.

Benetsee, now, he tells me about the coyote howling by the bones up the in that draw, tells me I'll figure it out when I see Coyote scratch the earth. They scratch the damn earth all the time. The old fart knows something. Probably everything. I think I don't want to talk to him.

Someday I'll be senile, won't know anything at all, whew.

Just like God, maybe He's senile.

Du Pré pulled up beside the old man. The drunken old fart was singing, high thin voice, Coyote French, love song for a voyageur's girl. Pull on the rope, bring me home. Benetsee was carrying a little bundle of dried flowers.

32

Du Pré rolled down the far window. "Want a ride?" he yelled.

Benetsee glanced at him, went off singing again, made an obscene gesture. No, and go do things to a lame coyote.

Du Pré shrugged, drove on. Now I got to go look for him at sunset, or maybe he freeze to death tonight. Damn.

Maria had the stove in the kitchen stoked up so it was red hot. It was so warm she was washing the dishes and cleaning up in a bra and panties. When she heard him come in she grabbed a robe, wrapped it around herself.

My daughter's a woman, good-looking, too, thought Du Pré. Ass like her mother's. Figures.

"You want something to eat," said Maria. "Billy brought us some venison, I got some other stuff at the store."

"Sure," said Du Pré. "Old Benetsee may show up. He's drunk."

"He's always drunk," said Maria.

"He bother you?"

Maria shook her head. "He's just like that, but a good man," she said. "Lots worse things to be than drunk."

"You want to talk to me?" said Du Pré. Make a stab at being a father, I don't know how.

Maria shook her head.

✤ CHAPTER 11 ✤

"That girl ever talk to you about the other night?" said Madelaine. She poured them coffee. Her children were off at school, except for the littlest, Sebastian, who had a cold. The kid kept coming into the kitchen, snuffling and sniveling.

"She don't need to talk," said Du Pré. "Thing about Maria is she's a good girl wants us to think she's bad."

"She needs a mother."

"She had one," said Du Pré. "Now all she got is me. And, Madelaine, I don't want you trying to mother her, it just upset both of you, and then, of course, it upset me."

"I just want to help."

"Sometimes the best help is no help at all."

Sebastian wandered back to his lonely bed of pain, a cookie in each chubby fist.

"See," said Du Pré, "when my wife was dying and she knew it and she made her peace with God and sent her love to her people and told me what to feed the dog and the cats. Took care of everything. So I took the little girls, four and eleven, into the big hospital in their little white dresses. Their eyes were very big, Mama was dying, she was going up to heaven, and my wife told me to leave the little girls with her a minute and go out into the hall and wait, she had to talk to them some, women things . . ."

Madelaine was looking very hard at her coffee, more than it deserved.

34

"So I went out in the hall and the little girls were in there for maybe fifteen minutes, I don't know. And my wife, she went into a coma that night and she never woke up. When she die, I have a house full of relatives, of course, and the priest, and all that, and I go out—it's summer, when she had that bad cold killed her—just to get away from all the people . . ."

Madelaine coughed some, sipped some coffee.

"So I'm sitting out there by the little creek, on a log, glad I don't have to hear someone tell me how sorry they are—I loved her a lot, you know, tore my insides out to lose her—and I looked up and there are my two little girls, one has a sandwich for me, the other a half-bottle of whiskey . . ."

Madelaine scratched her neck.

"So I say thank you, I eat the sandwich and have some of the whiskey, and Jacqueline says 'Mama told us to take care of you. So we do that. I'm older, so what I'm gonna do is get married soon as I can and have a lot of babies for all the babies that Mama couldn't have for you . . .' "

Du Pré choked up. He caught himself, went on. Madelaine took his hand.

"And then little Maria, who's four, says that while Jacqueline is busy having all those babies she'll take care of me just as good as Mama did, do a real good job for sure."

Madelaine squeezed Du Pré's hand.

"So they raised themselves always thinking got to take care of Papa, don't upset Papa. All I can do is not get upset with them. They have done very well, better than I could have done for them, if I knew what to do for them, which I don't, I think."

"They're jealous of me," murmured Madelaine.

"So you drop dead, Maria will fix her hair back and start

going to Mass and confession again," said Du Pré. "Not that I like the idea."

"I ain't going to drop dead," said Madelaine. "They don't need me mothering them, I guess."

"They might need it," said Du Pré, "but they won't have it."

"You've been a real good father to them."

"I keep my mouth shut, let them take care of me," said Du Pré. "Worst of it was to have a eleven-year-old and a four-year-old do all the cooking. Some of the things I ate, smiling, I still have bad dreams on. But they got better at it and I lived."

Madelaine laughed, a long deep throaty one.

"I'm jealous of them, too," said Madelaine.

"Why?" said Du Pré.

"They got some of you I can't have," said Madelaine, "and I got some of you they can't have."

"Sometimes I feel like a piece of salt-water taffy," said Du Pré.

"Poor Du Pré," said Madelaine dryly. "All these women fussing over him and he feels bad used."

Du Pré grinned. "Not a bad life," he said.

Madelaine yawned. She'd been up all night with Sebastian, in the rocking chair, holding him against the pain.

"I got to go," said Du Pré. "They're shipping some of those Crossed Eyes cattle, I got to sign off on them."

Madelaine nodded.

Du Pré leaned over and kissed her good-bye.

✤ CHAPTER 12 ✤

Du Pré watched the brands closely. Always. A steer was a wad of hundred-dollar bills on the hoof, and it always paid to run a few weren't yours on through. Anytime.

Bodie was out of jail and still limping. He took one look at Du Pré and went as far away as he could without quitting the ranch entire. He spat a lot.

Du Pré looked at the brand. Five fours any old line, couple slashes. Crossed Eyes would have been better. He wondered if the red face that had asked him who he was was strapped to a bed somewhere, screaming.

Shipping two hundred and thirteen head. The trucks backed up and loaded their forty or whatever, two tiers. B A A A A A A A W W W W L L L L L L L L L L L L L L L L. S S S H H H H H I I I I I I I I I I I I I I I I I T T T T.

Cows don't got much of an act, Du Pré thought.

Loaded up, Du Pré signed off. The cattle went down to Wyoming, someone had come into a little money and hated having it, bought cattle. Well, it always was a funny business.

Du Pré saw an old, old cowboy across the way, carrying a plastic sack of garbage to the slit trench where the offal was dumped, then covered with earth dumped by a backhoe every evening, or they would have skunks in numbers, and one skunk was plenty.

Booger Tom. That was the man's moniker. As opposed

to a name. Du Pré remembered him from the rodeos of his childhood. Booger Tom had seemed old then, helped in the chutes, too old to ride pickup or play the clown.

"Booger Tom!" Du Pré shouted, the old man was likely deaf.

The old cowboy stopped, stared over at Du Pré. Gabriel walked over to him, hand out.

"Why, if it ain't Gabriel Du Pré," he said. "You're old Catfoot's boy. Yes, well, I ain't seen you in years."

They talked of nothing much, the water or lack of it, weather, dust, cattle, a few men now dead they both had known.

"You always work here?" said Du Pré.

"Forty year. Worked for the Higginses, then these people," Tom said, spitting in the dirt, these people. "Get to my age, it's hard to get work."

"When did Higgins sell this place," asked Du Pré. His mind was prickling.

"Sixty-eight," said Booger Tom.

Gabriel nodded. Maybe. Time was a little close, though.

"But these Fascellis, they leased the place starting in sixty-two . . . waited a while to drop the hammer."

Du Pré's mind prickled a lot.

"Well, who owns it now?" He looked up at the Wolfs.

"Them kids, old man Fascelli died. Them two in the house are his son and daughter. But they ain't around even if they are. They drink. Their mother's in a nursing home. Checks come out of Dee-troyt. Regular about that, anyway."

"Well," said Du Pré, "they seem to be having a lot of fun I guess you'd call it. Jesus."

Booger Tom looked up at the ridiculous house with an old and rarefied hatred.

"When they first come here there was four of them

kids," said Booger Tom, "all wild, now there's just the two."

The fat red face Du Pré recalled staggered out of the front door of the gross house, lurching like his feet had forgot where his body was. The man found a lawn chair and fell into it. He turned to the house and yelled something Du Pré couldn't make out. A maid hurried to him, bearing a tray with bottles and an ice bucket on it.

"I got to go," said Booger Tom, staring hard at the drunk.

Du Pré started walking to the man sprawled in the lawn chair. He was drinking something brown out of a tall glass, and spilling it on his shirt. Shaking his head as though confused.

But by the time that Du Pré got there he was cold sober.

"May I help you?" he said pleasantly.

"Gabriel Du Pré," said Du Pré. "I just inspected the brands on your cattle. All in order, too, I signed off on them."

"I should hope so," said the man. "Drink?" He waved a red hand at the tray, the bottles, his life.

Gabriel nodded. The man put a double slug into a glass, added ice and water, handed it up.

"I'm Bart Fascelli," said the man, offering his hand.

The change fascinated Du Pré.

Gabriel shook the hand.

"So," said Fascelli, "you inspect brands. Do you know horses?"

"A little."

"Come and look at my pasofinos."

He led Gabriel to the horse barn, a new one, white with blue trim. It would have looked good on some millionaire's racing farm, in Kentucky, here it looked like it dropped from the moon.

They talked about horses. Then Bart walked Gabriel to his car.

"Come anytime," said Fascelli, his big red hands on the window.

Du Pré nodded and drove away.

"Now what's this shit about?" he said aloud.

A woolly bear caterpillar crawled across the dashboard. The orange band was wide.

Sign of a hard winter, some said.

❧ CHAPTER 13 ❧

Du Pré stood up and cheered loudly. Maria had just sunk a long jump shot and put her team ahead. The girls raced downcourt, set themselves in their defense. The crowd was fiercely partisan. Three fights had already broken out.

Girls' basketball. They were fast and graceful. This was fairly new, Du Pré thought, all them years when no one taught girls to move their arms when they run or shoot a basketball. They were good, damn good, and much fun to watch.

"Look at them now," said Madelaine. "These girls, they are very good. Your daughter, she's the star, see her shoot!"

Madelaine's oldest, Suzanne, was the center. Tall, like her vanished father.

Toussaint had no high school, the kids went to Cooper, the other team was from Fort Benton. Better team, lots more kids to pick from.

The breeds yell for Toussaint, the whites yell for Cooper, same team, Du Pré thought. What a bunch of fools we all are.

Maria fouled out. Du Pré saw her roached hair in some sort of cartoon whirligig, he expected to see dust, fist here, head there. She always fouled out. The Crusher, her teammates called her.

"My daughter, she take life very seriously," Du Pré muttered.

"What?" said Madelaine.

I don't understand any of my women, even when I do.

"Nothing," said Du Pré. He muttered to himself, came of working alone, someone to talk to.

Madelaine huffled, mad he wouldn't tell her.

"Du Pré," said Madelaine, "you go talk to your daughter, there."

Maria was on the bench, slumped over with her head in her hands.

Du Pré picked his way down the creaky bleachers.

"Child," he said, behind her, his hand on her shoulder. Maria turned. She had been crying. Her eyes crinkled up.

"I wanna play football, sack quarterbacks," she said.

Du Pré touched a bruise on her forehead, right above the eyebrow.

"You go sit there," said Maria, "right there." She pointed to an empty spot on the bleachers behind her. Du Pré sat. She walked round the bench and came and sat next to him, leaned against him. She smelled fresh, young sweat without much sin in it.

They watched her team lose.

"We wait for you, buy you a pop or something," said Du Pré. "Now where is Billy?" He looked back for the boy.

Maria shrugged. Billy was not doing good with her, for sure.

41

"Well," said Du Pré, "you want the pop or you got more fun folks to be with?"

"I bother Madelaine," said Maria.

"She bother you."

"S'pose I ought to learn to put up with her," said Maria.

"Hey, make it easy on your papa. Damn women anyway."

Maria laughed and went off to the showers.

Du Pré and Madelaine stood waiting for their children. Other parents slapped backs, exchanged dinner invitations, replayed the game, the shots, the errors.

Two men began shouting and swinging at each other.

Maria came out first, scruffy clothes, torn jeans, cheap boots that crumpled around her ankles, one papier-mâché earring. All clean, mind you. Du Pré wondered if she broke her clothes in with a hatchet.

"I want to go dancing," said Maria, "but there's no place to go."

"Who you gonna dance with?" said Du Pré. "Since Billy's went missing?"

"Myself alone," said Maria. Whatever the trouble, she was really mad with him. Billy should switch on his old truck, suck the tailpipe good and hard.

"OK," said Du Pré. "You dance with your old fart father, bar in Toussaint's got a jukebox."

Suzanne's fella was waiting on her, glands visibly throbbing.

Du Pré, Madelaine, and Maria got into the old cruiser and he drove to the bar in Toussaint. They took a little table and Gabriel bought soda for Maria, pink wine for Madelaine, whiskey for himself.

Du Pré danced with his daughter, danced with Madelaine, and then Maria danced by herself. A young half-drunk cowboy asked to join her. She nodded. The two

42

slouched together on the slow songs, danced far apart on the fast ones.

Du Pré walked out to Maria, nodded to the cowboy. "I got to go and you got to come with me," he said. The bar rules were that children were OK, but with a parent and no booze for them.

After they had dropped Maria off, Madelaine asked to go back to the bar for one or two more. Du Pré nodded. He was tired but not sleepy.

I'm listening to a record, he thought, the needle is whispering over the blank grooves, the song hasn't started yet.

But could you dance to it? Have fun?

The Toussaint bar was empty, the woman behind the worn bartop was washing up. Madelaine sat down at a table, Du Pré went to the bar, got a couple for them.

"This all right?" said Madelaine. "You pretty tired. We don't got to stay long."

Du Pré shook his head. "Just a little tired but not sleepy," he said.

Benetsee shuffled out of the men's room. He came over and stood for a moment, swaying a little.

The old man reached in his coat pocket and pulled out a knife, one mostly gone to rust. The elkhorn handle had been gnawed by pack rats.

"This was up in the wall of your shed, there," said Benetsee.

Du Pré picked it up. Handmade. Catfoot used to make knives. Knives for everything. He had more than fifty, Du Pré remembered. Made them out of old sawmill band saw steel.

The knife blade had a skin hook on the tip, a thick curved blade. Half of the top was toothed. Catfoot could skin out a deer, use the saw blade to saw through the joints in minutes.

Benetsee shuffled out the door.

Du Pré slipped the knife into his pocket.

Good steel, he thought.

Benetsee, he is telling me something.

What?

✦ CHAPTER 14 ✦

Bart Fascelli sat well on his horse. He shrugged inside his long slicker, taking the binds out before riding. Du Pré looked away. Was this the man who had screamed at him from the window?

He was sober now. He had called, wanted to see the place where Bodie had found the wreck. In the rain. He offered to pay Du Pré but Gabriel had refused.

I just listen, that song, someday I know all the words, Du Pré thought.

A maid came out of the house, she had a pair of saddle-bags, one in each hand. She wore just a thin white uniform, hunched herself against the splacking drops.

Probably snowing up there, the Wolfs, but it was early, not like the last time, they'd have light to make camp in.

Du Pré tied the bags behind him, they were fairly heavy. Du Pré wondered if there was a portable sauna in one of them. But Fascelli was sober, no reek of alcohol. Even if he'd been drinking yesterday he'd still smell.

Du Pré couldn't figure him out. He had a twin brother, maybe?

No.

There were two Barts. Maybe more. Time to time he went off his head. Did he want to go up there, see if he remembered it? When he had a sack across his horse? A sack that dripped little streaks of watery red?

So we go to a place of death and puzzles. Du Pré remembered Catfoot taking him, a child, to an old battleground, the air was sad there, Du Pré had been frightened. A place of bad hearts.

He crossed himself, felt the lump in his shirt pocket.

The shrew skull in the coyote scat. Du Pré had put the hairy turd in a little black plastic box, one that once held a hundred rounds of .22 ammunition. Gopher loads.

I don't think I probably want to know the answer to all this but I'm going to out anyway, Du Pré thought. A small cascade of icy water sluiced off his hat, onto the narrow strip of skin between his sleeve and glove. He moved his hand out of the way. The horse chuffled, swung his head, Du Pré had bumped the bit a little.

Du Pré clucked to the horse, a fine-gaited pasofino. Little, but tough. He wondered how much the horse cost. Bart wouldn't care about that. Why did he care about this?

They got to the foothills, Bart pulled up, swung down, put his hands in the small of his back and stretched. Snow clouds were huddled against the peaks. It would be damn wet and cold up there, the kind of wet weather kills people. Hypothermia. Eats flatlander backpackers. Not often enough. All the streams were polluted with *Giardia* now, the ninnies always brought their dogs, the better to spread it further.

"Some country, isn't it?" said Bart, banging one gloved hand into the other.

"All I know," said Du Pré, "but I like it pretty good."

"That plane went down in . . . 1959?" Bart asked.

45

"Fifty-seven," said Du Pré. Bart was close. These Fascellis, they came in '62. Did he come up here in '62, young then, on fire for the mountains? Find the wreck, keep it close against his need?

Long damn time for all these questions to wait.

Du Pré wondered why something kept nibbling out on the edge of his mind, telling him he didn't really want to know about this one. But he had to know now, even if he didn't want to.

Bart swung back up, headed up the trail. At the gate in the high fence he got down, opened the lock, swung the green pipe gate back to let Du Pré through. Gabriel reached for the other horse's reins and tugged the horse along. Bart locked up, swung up, they went on.

He was in good shape, for sure. Bad drunks now, their muscles melt away and they shake, too weak to do anything close to this.

They rode up into timber. A grouse banged off beneath Bart's horse. The animal skittered a little, Bart calmed him, another grouse boomed away from a bush. But the horse was used to them now, didn't even snort.

"You lead," said Bart, moving off the trial. "Where is it anyway?"

"Three miles, maybe four," said Du Pré.

"You think Bodie is stupid?" said Bart.

"Very," said Du Pré. "He's a bad hand with stock. You should fire him. He hurts them."

"Consider it done," said Bart.

"Booger Tom work for you all these years, eh?"

Bart nodded. "He's a nice old man, allowing for cowboy quirks. I like him, he hates us, how could he not? Rich, drunken assholes is what we are."

Du Pré looked away. What about this?

"Runs in the family," said Bart. "We aren't smart

enough to be artists. We could get away with a lot more if we were."

Du Pré laughed. He was beginning to like this Bart. The other Bart was a bastard and he hadn't met the rest.

Du Pré flicked his eyes left, right, up, looking for sign, the leaf without the raindrops on it, the shadow in the grass where feet had pressed it down, the branch swaying wrong, where the eagle had lifted off, great wings beating.

They came to the little meadow at the foot of the draw. Du Pré saw a pile of duffel, a big tent all up and taut.

The place where the helicopter had landed.

"I'm staying up here a few days, maybe," said Bart. "Had this stuff flown on up. You do what you want, but I need to stay."

Du Pré looked at him.

"Why you need me to bring you up here for, you knew where it was already?" I got work to do, this ain't it, for sure.

"I didn't really," said Bart. "The flying service just landed these things for me where they came before. I need you to show me where the wreck was, of course."

"OK," said Du Pré. Must be nice, call a helicopter to do the heavy work, say send me the bill.

They grained the horses, hobbled them, turned them loose.

Du Pré led Bart up the draw.

The trail was slick and wet, their boots were not much good for hiking, high heels, slick soles.

They sweated inside their slickers. When they opened them to cool down, their shirts steamed.

❖ CHAPTER 15 ❖

D u Pré stood by the hole in the ground where the little engine had been. The earth had been turned and raked, looking for bits and pieces. They had waved metal detectors, sifted, a lot of hours.

"The plane hit up there," said Du Pré, pointing. The yellow scar on the gray rock was barely visible through the light rain.

"Quick, anyway," said Bart. He walked round, hands in his pockets. The little watercourse was chuckling with runoff. Stunted chokecherry bushes lined the sides of the stream. The place where Du Pré had found the skull was a foot under water.

"It'll snow tonight," said Du Pré. The air smelled of it, and snow was falling hard up higher.

"Tore it up, didn't they?" said Bart. The FAA people had been very thorough. Du Pré could see where someone had even rappelled down the rock face, to measure the scar on the rock. Thirty-odd years and it still showed yellow. These mountains, they rotted very slowly.

But rot they did.

"You going to stay tonight," said Bart, coughing.

"Yes," said Du Pré. Why not, I can't read this man, make anything of him. What do I know to be true about this all?

What in the hell happened here, exactly? And why?

Du Pré rolled a cigarette, flicked his lighter to flame. His

48

mustache was wet. The cigarette turned brown. He cursed and threw the sodden butt away.

Bart pissed. The yellow stream steamed, white tendrils.

"I'm just going to wander around," he said. He walked up the path, stooping from time to time.

Du Pré always thought he could think better if he was moving, it probably was just foolishness, like most of life. In a little patch of grass and brush near him he saw a smooth, rounded boulder, a kind of rock from someplace else to the north. The glaciers had covered this place long ago, and crept down from Canada carrying pieces of other mountains in their guts. A close-grained reddish stone, with black mica in it.

Du Pré wondered how far it had come.

The FAA people hadn't cast out this far, the grass hadn't seen a foot on it. Du Pré went to the rock, sat on it, felt the cold through his slicker and jeans. He tilted forward, unbuttoned his slicker, brought out his tobacco pouch, rolled a cigarette, wiped his mustache hard. He lit the smoke, hid under his hatbrim, back to the little wind.

The Olesons ship their stock the day after tomorrow. So I'll go back in the morning, see Madelaine, get a piece of her sweet ass.

He dropped the cigarette. The butt hissed in the wet sparse grass, brown stains shot through the paper, it went out. Du Pré stared at it idly.

A little fleck of white down there between his boots. He poked at it with a finger. A tooth. With a filling in it.

Another one, white with dried brown roots.

Du Pré slipped his pocketknife out of his pants, dug carefully Three more. One had a filling in it, too. Hoo boy.

Du Pré put the teeth in his shirt pocket, next to the little box with the coyote scat. He snapped the flap.

Now what about this?

Whoever hauled that head up here had used this stone for an anvil, knocked the teeth out of the head, probably pounded most of them to dust but these got lost.

Was it coming on dark?

Maybe the guy was working drunk.

Now I got to tell the Sheriff. Now we got a little more, maybe the Headless Man begins to speak.

Or maybe a drunk just fell on this rock, knocked out his teeth.

But these are molars.

The rain ran off Du Pré's hat, a filmy sheet.

Du Pré saw a flash of movement off at the edge of his vision. He turned his head, slowly. A coyote, yellow-gray. The animal's head snapped up. Du Pré had been sitting still thinking and the wet held his scent close.

The coyote was gone, like so much smoke.

God's dogs, the Cree called them. Smart sonsofbitches. Du Pré had seen one robbing a bees' nest once, big clumsy bumblebees. The coyote had waved his thick tail at the nest, the bees attacked it. Then the coyote had turned slowly, the bees kept after his tail, and the coyote gobbled down the honey and larva while the poor bees tried to sting through five inches of fur on the tail. Poor, dumb bees.

I feel like them bees with this murder, here. I'm probably after the wrong end.

Du Pré heard a small plane snarling overhead. In this muck? Better be above it.

Du Pré stood up. He looked again where the coyote had been. The animal was long gone, and surely looking back at Du Pré from some safe and hidden place.

When I die, Du Pré thought, I want to come back as a coyote. If they *are* God's dogs they must know about everything important. Me, I tell my dog everything.

I like it when they sing.

✤ CHAPTER 16 ✤

The snow rattled on the tent, the size of little hard kernels of corn.

First time that I have eaten caviar in the wilderness, Gabriel thought. First time. Catfoot used to make good caviar from them paddlefish eggs. This stuff comes from Russia. Probably even up trade, ounce of gold, ounce of caviar.

And I am liking Bart here. He needs a job. Maybe I tell him, Bart, just sneak off, ride the rods to Portland, get a job as a dishwasher, you'd be happier. Get killed by another hobo on the way, you'd be happier than you are now.

Du Pré was sipping whiskey. Bart was drinking pop. His face wasn't red, he didn't look like he had hanging out the window, cursing.

We all need something to do. Trouble was, Bart would think he had to be the best at whatever he did, make up for the rest of his life. Me, I'm glad I didn't have money waiting on me.

"You like that caviar, eh?" Bart said, grinning. In there, a generous man, really.

Du Pré nodded. "I make some a little different, out of the paddlefish eggs. Put just a touch of the hot pepper sauce in them. The eggs are a little bigger, not much."

"What in the hell is a paddlefish?"

Du Pré described the big fish, sometimes a hundred and fifty pounds, he'd heard it was a relative of the sturgeon.

Catch them in the Missouri, the Yellowstone. Bottom feeders, mussels, crawfish, what have you. Maybe stirred the bottom with the paddle on its nose.

"Makes his own caviar," Bart murmured. He stared off far away to someplace cold.

"I barely know how to do anything," he said finally. "My résumé would be short. Drink. Write checks."

Suddenly he grew agitated, scratched himself. Closed his eyes and shivered. When he opened his eyes they weren't the same eyes, they were darker and very desperate. He scrabbled in the box where he had the booze. Lifted out a fifth of vodka, chugged half of it down, choked and heaved, forcing himself not to throw up. Then he sat back, eyes closed again. His hands gripped folds of his trousers. The tendons stood out, practically twanging.

Du Pré watched, wondered. The poor son of a bitch.

Bart let his breath out slowly. His eyes opened.

"Happens when I go off it," he said, "about the third day. Docs tell me I'll die of it sometime. Heart attack or seizure or something. If I jerk and foam, just leave me alone. It would be better than this."

Du Pré nodded. Well, Bart had the comfort of knowing the manner of his death. You could get used to it some that way.

A sudden bash of wind slammed into the tent, lifted the uphill side, nearly blew the thing over. Cold air knifed through. Du Pré buttoned his down vest.

Du Pré rolled himself a cigarette, lit it, didn't look at Bart. Maybe I end up riding down the mountain tonight. He remembered where the ax was, outside, buried in a stump. What do I know about this?

Du Pré had seen a lot of crazy drunks but they always got nuts after they had been drinking for days. But no one he knew had enough money to do that very often. You got the

D.T.'s, dried out, went back on the job. But this poor guy was a real pro, some life.

Bart cooked steaks on a gas grill. Fresh asparagus.

Du Pré had spent a lot of time up in the mountains, but the menu had been jerky, sardines, fruit leather, tea. Maybe rabbit.

Bart opened a bottle of red wine from France. It was very good. Probably sold for the same price as Du Pré's house, a case of it.

"I'll be OK now," said Bart. "I didn't find anything much up there. Did you?"

Du Pré shook his head, scratched the teeth through the cloth of his shirt.

"Your family all gone?" said Du Pré. Probably better they were.

"Well, mostly," said Bart. "Father and mother dead. One sister lives down in that house with me. She's worse'n I am. Hires studs, flies them out. Other sister went straight, sober, she's in Seattle works as a counselor there, alcohol. My brother died a long time ago."

Du Pré's ears pricked, went up, like a coyote's. He thought he heard one howl. In the blowing snow? They howl when they hunt, try to scare up a rabbit. But not in blowing snow.

Blowing snow, they try to sneak up on grouse buried in the drifts. Get hungry, get bold, go down and cut a sheep out of the flocks. Though not so much now the ranchers using those dogs, Maremmas, those others look to be all covered in noodles.

"He just disappeared from Chicago," Bart went on. "Last seen at the airport, had a flight to Denver. We thought he might have come up here, but he didn't. Never a trace."

53

"He sick like you?" Du Pré wanted to bite his tongue.

"Gianni? I don't know. Maybe he hadn't been at it long enough. All I remember is he had his appendix out. Sixteen or so."

Du Pré thought on that one, gummed it round. Lots of people have their appendix out. The Headless Man did, for one.

They talked of nothing much, slept.

In the morning Du Pré had coffee, saddled up. The cold leather creaked, snow bowed the firs down.

"You want me to take your horse, send the helicopter for you?" Du Pré said.

Bart nodded. He was a little shaky, pulling on tomato juice with a lot of vodka in it.

"Please take the horse," he said, looking close to tears. "But don't have the helicopter come for a couple days. I don't want to go back down at all, truth to tell. Couple days, I'll be all right."

"You not going to be all right, do this," said Du Pré.

Bart nodded.

But he didn't want to talk any more.

♣ CHAPTER 17 ♣

Yeah," said Du Pré, "he about shit I told him all that."
Madelaine swirled her sweet pink wine in the glass. She smiled, looked up at Du Pré.

"What did he do with the teeth?"

"Last I saw, he was looking at the teeth, they was sitting

on his desk, he was dialing on the telephone. I am out of it. I don't want any more."

"And Foosli is still up there?"

"Fascelli? Yes. I don't know. I feel damn sorry for that poor son of a bitch. Here's Foosli one minute, next he's gone. Fascelli, I mean, damn you."

Maria brought her hamburger to the table. She sat, demurely spread her lap with paper napkins. Still the torn black jeans. Du Pré wondered maybe she wanted part of her bad ass hang out of it.

"What happened to this counselor you had to go see?" said Du Pré. Used to be, kid get caught with beer, they got yelled at by a cop, parents made them stay home for a while, dance with the chickens. Now they got lame social workers all over them. No wonder they're more homicidal.

Government peckerwood wants to help, that *never* add up.

Maria shrugged, wrinkled her face like she had a bad smell under her pretty nose.

"He wanted to know you molest me or something," said Maria, she looked down. She was laughing.

"WHAT!"

Du Pré stood up, white with rage. Who the hell are these people anyway?

"So I told him lie down on the floor, suck himself," said Maria, "and I walked out."

My child, my child, thought Du Pré, now she tell me who I got to kill.

"You really say that to the man?" said Madelaine. She was trying to look shocked.

"I really say that to the man."

"What he say?"

"Nothing. I holler back that I tell my papa he ask me

such a filthy question my papa probably blow his shit brains out."

"Where this guy come from, anyway?" said Du Pré, steaming good.

"It's Bucky Dassault."

"Bucky Dassault! Jesus, that drunk? He maybe get arrested, drunk driving a hundred times, rape his sister once."

"I know," said Maria. "He go off to Galen, get a certificate, now he wants to help. Everything he done the bad alcohol and drugs make him do. Now he's sober, he says, wants to help."

"Well, you tell him," said Madelaine. She drank her pink wine.

"I tell him. Damn, he's a piece of shit drunk or sober, now he got a counselor's job. He's a *professional* . . ."

Du Pré sat back down. He wanted to start strangling people right away, begin with Bucky Dassault, end with the governor, not miss anyone in between.

"Du Pré," said Madelaine, "calm down, she already tear his balls off."

"So what I do with that bullshit, heh?" said Maria.

"What bullshit?" said Du Pré.

"Judge say I got to go talk to Bucky Dassault, go to AA for a while. Otherwise he send me to some place the state run to help me."

"How come this is the first I hear of it?" said Du Pré.

"Because I tell these assholes they talk like that to me in front of my daddy he probably kill them, scalp them, piss on what's left."

"I take care of it," said Du Pré.

"I don't want you to take care of it, Du Pré," said Madelaine. "I don't want to have come see you in Deer Lodge."

"Well, I go see that damn judge for sure," said Du Pré. He knew the guy, used to be a lousy prosecutor, always getting things wrong. Now he's a JP, way things going he be moving up to the Supreme Court next week. The one in D.C.

My daughter's a fine young woman, kids with beer, like kids ever and for always, now it's a big fucking deal. These people can't lie on the ground without a law says they have to.

Guy tries to kill me, I shoot up his arm, he gets a suspended sentence on account of his shot-up arm. My daughter gets busted with some beer, she gets gang-banged by a bunch of assholes ought to be hung 'cause they dumb and ugly. Shit.

Du Pré drove Madelaine home, took Maria out to the house. He thought he'd sleep there tonight, take her with him in the morning, straighten this thing out.

"Du Pré," said Madelaine, "you watch your temper, hear? When Albert run off, I had to get food stamps for a while, you wouldn't believe the shit I had to go through to get them. Them social worker people are crazy and worthless and they know it, know you know it."

"What is all this?" said Du Pré, pounding his hands on the steering wheel.

"We women, we're used to eating shit," said Madelaine. "You go careful tomorrow, that dumb judge throw you in jail for thinking he's dumb."

At home, Du Pré sat out on the porch in the cold. He was very hot and when he was mad he burned.

"Papa," said Maria from the doorway, "I know you can't sleep. Here you drink this, please, for me."

She handed him a tall glass, hot water, whiskey, a little lemon.

"I'm going to bed now," said Maria. "I think I won't go with you tomorrow."

"Why the hell not?" said Du Pré.

"Well," said Maria, "if I am right there and they get snotty, you get really mad. You don't have me there to protect, maybe you don't get so mad."

Du Pré nodded.

My child, she take good care of me.

❧ CHAPTER 18 ❧

Bucky Dassault wore the smarmy look of the saved. Once he was blind, and now he had an office and a diploma and a steady supply of people to mess with and fuck up, and he was a very happy asshole with a lot of undeserved clout. A Pro-Fess-ional, like Maria said.

Why the fuck don't we take fucking Charley Manson, Du Pré seethed, make him director of social services. He had a lousy childhood, you see. This would make him extra helpful to troubled folks.

Du Pré was very calm. Bucky was not fooled.

"It's the law," said Bucky.

Du Pré looked at him, didn't say anything.

"Du Pré, the State of Montana takes alcohol and drug abuse very seriously."

"Then why they hire you," said Du Pré, "they take it seriously?"

"Du Pré . . ."

"You were a piece of shit born and I don't think much

changed," said Du Pré. "Leave my daughter alone. I don't tell you that again."

Du Pré left. He thought about getting drunk before going to see this jerk judge, judge throw him in jail for contempt, sentence him to go talk to Bucky . . . Deer Lodge Prison, sure.

The food there was very lousy, no pussy, Du Pré would hate it.

Government, they can't do anything right.

Any self-respecting kid sneaks off, do some beer, smoke some dope. Now it's a big damn deal, got professionals for it. Like goddamned Bucky Dassault. I kick his ass I get thrown in jail, which make me so mad I will kill him.

My daughter's raising herself just fine, spite of my best effort and that is all a kid ought to have to put up with.

Du Pré ran into the Sheriff at the courthouse in Cooper. The big loud cop was there to testify in a drunk driving case.

"Guy hit a car," said the Sheriff. "Bounced up on my sidewalk, through my hedge, stopped with the hood all folded around a tree in my yard, fer Chrissakes. Three o'clock in the morning."

The Sheriff had made his own arrest. Call "60 Minutes."

"What are you here for?" he said, looking at Du Pré.

"My daughter was partying with some kids, had some beer, got caught, now they want to make her go listen to Bucky Dassault. Attend AA. She already goes to Mass. I am damn mad."

"The Judge is a pussy," said the Sheriff. "Don't scare him."

So Du Pré kept his mouth shut. Good thing, too. The Pussy Judge did all his talking for him anyway.

"Ssssince you are in . . . Lawn Forcement . . . waive . . .

to your custody . . . don't want to see her here again . . . serious matter," said the Pussy Judge.

This so fucking serious, why that damn Bucky Dassault, thought Du Pré, while he looked respectful.

Du Pré said he took the whole matter very seriously.

The Pussy Judge went on to other matters, just before Du Pré would have lost his temper he had to stand and listen to any more of this bullshit. Which would have been tragic for everybody.

Du Pré asked God Who the Fuck was Minding the Store outside on the sidewalk. What the hell ever happened to kids will be kids, and kids do this sort of thing, practicing to be screwed-up adults like everybody else? Huh?

Du Pré drove back to Toussaint, sat in the bar which was empty except for the lady with the beehive hairdo who was washing everything. Du Pré drank whiskey, wished someone would come in he could kill—a Texan would be nice, can't get convicted of killing a Texan in Montana. Maybe I go find a dog with a calloused butt and kick him.

The telephone rang, the lady at the bar looked at Du Pré. She pointed at the pay phone on the wall by the front door. Du Pré walked over to it, picked it up.

"Papa," said Maria, "are you all right?"

"I just pissed off," said Du Pré. "All these people butting in business isn't any of theirs. Anyway, you don't have to go and talk to that damn Bucky Dassault or any of the rest of that crap. But you not to get caught again, you hear? I don't think it a bad thing that kids drink beer, long as they don't drive around. But now you got a bunch of bad people paid by the government to mess with you, call it help, and that is a lot of trouble."

"I know," said Maria. "I get caught with beer again my papa gets sent to prison." She laughed. So did Du Pré.

"I love you, Papa," she said.

60

"Love you too," said Du Pré. "Hey, I come and get you, we get Madelaine, we eat dinner here maybe."

"I pick up Madelaine," said Maria. Du Pré considered the fact that his daughter now had a car and a driver's license, or anyway a car. Du Pré, shut up, he told himself.

"OK," said Du Pré.

I know I don't do this father job so good, so I wish you luck, Maria.

"When you get this car?" said Du Pré.

"I love you, Papa," said Maria, hanging up.

Maria came to the bar alone. Madelaine was feeding her kids, she would come when they were cared for.

"Where'd you get the car?" said Du Pré, trying.

"Let's dance," said Maria. She put money in the jukebox.

♣ CHAPTER 19 ♣

It has to be the Headless Man," said the Sheriff, "the report says the teeth have fillings in them and appear weathered."

"Very interesting," said Du Pré. "I got back to inspecting cattle right now. I got five shipments here, four there, I am a very busy brand inspector." All yours, Jack.

"Where'd they bury the Headless Man, anyway?" asked the Sheriff.

"I don't know," said Du Pré. "Potter's field, maybe."

"Never heard of it," said the Sheriff.

"It's back of the old Mission church in Toussaint," said

Du Pré. "Where all the drunks freeze to death their families too poor to bury buried."

"Why there?"

"What?"

"Why behind the Catholic church?"

"The poor people around here are mostly Catholic," said Du Pré.

"Are you Met-isse?"

Du Pré nodded.

"Well, what are they? Indians?"

This son of a bitch here since '75 and he don't know what Métis are, Du Pré thought. "Red River breeds. they come down here after the Rebellion in 1886, some come before, this was the old buffalo hunting grounds. Come down in their Red River carts, get winter meat. The Métis were Cree and French, little English maybe. You know all them stories about the *voyageurs*? Métis."

"What rebellion?" said the Sheriff. "I thought the Red River was in Texas or something. John Wayne did a movie, yeah."

Du Pré had seen it, pretty good movie.

"Red River of the North," said Du Pré, "flows to Hudson Bay. See, I think the Missouri only flow like it does now since the last glaciers, ten thousand years or so. It used to flow into the Red River of the North."

"Red River Rebellion?"

So Du Pré told him about poor crazy Louis Riel, the saint, who led the rebellion and the English hung him. About little Gabriel Dumont, Riel's general, who would have destroyed the British troops but Jesus told Riel not to let Gabriel do it. The priests betrayed Riel to the English, Dumont tried to rescue Riel, bring him down to Montana. So for all his days thereafter Gabriel Dumont never once again spoke to priests.

62

So the Métis come here. Big families, couple horses, little blankets, a kettle, a wooden plow, a hoe, an ax.

"We still here," said Du Pré. "Still poor, still Catholic."

He left the Sheriff, drove off to his first inspection, small one, but he wanted to take his time. He didn't exactly think that the rancher was a thief, but he didn't exactly think that he wasn't, either.

He found them ready, a couple of stock haulers waiting. They ran the cattle by him, the brands looked OK, except for two might have been worked over a little.

"My youngest sort of screwed them up," said the rancher. "Had to touch up these two later . . ."

The story sounded OK, didn't sound OK, maybe, maybe not, was it worth skinning the steers, seeing what the original brand was. Du Pré subtracted the added scars, couldn't come up with a brand he knew.

Du Pré nodded. Not enough right now, but if someone came up missing a few head he'd be on this guy. He was half on him now. But you can't say "Judge, I have this feeling . . ."

"OK," said Du Pré, "everything's in order."

Or maybe the kid did screw them up, I'm just out of order.

The rancher tucked a chew in his lip.

"Du Pré," said the rancher, "seen in the Tribune about you finding that plane wreck and the rest of the Headless Man. Said you thought that the killer would be found pretty soon."

Du Pré nodded. That asshole reporter, don't get the quotes right that he likes, he makes them up.

"How's the investigation going? Any suspects?"

Television. What did those new shows call bad guys? Perps?

Jesus.

"I didn't say that," said Du Pré. "I don't know what the Sheriff is doing." Neither does the Sheriff.

"Oh."

"I look at cow asses," said Du Pré. "They just didn't have anybody to send so I went. I don't know much."

"Oh."

"Well," said Du Pré, "I got to go."

"Want some coffee?"

"No, I got another shipment, I got to run."

Du Pré drove away.

Perps.

Shit.

The next three shipments were all out of the same corrals, small lots of fifty or a hundred head. And a banker waiting to take the checks from the cattle buyer. Guy in lizardskin boots. Some banker.

The ranchers were going under, for sure, all working as long-haul truckers, just raising a few cows because that's what they'd always done. The brands were all good, Du Pré had known these people all his life.

He drove off to the last loading, some ten miles away. One of the bigger outfits, out-of-state money, probably a tax dodge.

Du Pré nodded at the foreman. He'd busted the man once. Before the man lost the ranch he tried one year to slip forty head of someone else's cattle past Du Pré. Well, it is pretty easy to spot bright new scar tissue, hardly had the scabs off, hard to sketch in a forged brand with a running iron and get the size right.

The man did a little time without complaint, and was always courteous to Du Pré.

Du Pré hadn't liked busting the guy. Now some assholes the government paid to lose money on cattle had the man's place. Including the little graveyard where his folks were buried.

The foreman lost the place, lost his money, worked for someone else on his family's land. Made that one try, he'd have done better to rob a bank, maybe.

The cattle marched past. Du Pré had to look hard at only one brand, had a bad tear across it, probably the animal fell onto a sharp rock or something. Just a rip across the brand, I know that's OK.

"Thanks, Du Pré," said the foreman, when Du Pré signed off.

"You bet, Jim," said Du Pré.

I still feel bad about busting him, thought Du Pré as he drove off. I always will.

♣ CHAPTER 20 ♣

Du Pré pulled his car over to a turnout on the dirt road, high up on the Bench, to look down the high plains toward Toussaint and Cooper and the blue haze beyond. He could see fifty miles south and east from the shoulders of the Wolf Mountains.

He rolled a cigarette, lit it, walked to the edge of the scraped dirt where the fireweed rattled. Late fall, soon on winter. Hadn't had a winter in a long time, but the summer had been cool and wet.

The winter right after the poor Métis fled south to escape the wrath of the English was the worst anyone remembered, 1886–87. That year there was no summer, two springs, the lilacs bloomed twice, some said because of the eruption of the volcano Krakatoa in the East Indies.

In December the winds howled high overhead, the air unstirred on the ground. The sky was pale gray and glittered. Snow began to fall, snow so fine that the cattle and horses inhaled it and froze their lungs and died of pneumonia. The temperature dropped to forty, fifty, sixty degrees below zero.

Then the Blizzard came.

The winds came.

Coulees a hundred feet deep filled with snow. Cattle wandered out into the flat white, sank into fluff. In the spring, the tops of the cottonwood trees had dead cattle in the forks of the branches.

Ninety percent of the range cattle in Montana died. The Texas herds had overgrazed the plains, too, so the cattle went into the winter lean and weak.

The Métis huddled in their tiny cabins, boiled moccasins for thin, stinking soup.

Corpses were stacked in the woodsheds, the ground was frozen many feet down.

Hard winter. There would be another someday.

Du Pré spat. He pissed, looking down at a couple of pickups racketing along the low road, one had a horse in back. Drivers were going too fast but everybody did here, you'd never get anywhere if you didn't.

I drive too fast. Now where the hell is Benetsee? The old man came and went, dropped his riddles. The old fart knows something. If the Headless Man is Gianni Fascelli, is who killed him down there right now? Could I see him if I had my binoculars?

Play my fiddle at midnight in the graveyard, summon up the Headless Man, have him tell me who? And this Headless Man, what would he speak with?

A rifle sounded, far away. Up in the mountains. All the hunters from the Flat States come here, think the game feeds on the snow up top of the peaks or something. Very little game up there in the deep green trees. Nothing for them to eat. Down here, there is a lot for them to eat. The haystacks of ranchers, for one.

I ought to go hunt this weekend, make winter meat.

When Gabriel Dumont led the buffalo hunt, he wore his red sash. I'll wear my red sash.

Benetsee. The prophets must have been a lot like him. No damn wonder folks killed them. Irritating sonsof-bitches.

Where had Benetsee gone? Some city, sleeping in door-ways in his old clothes, begging quarters?

I could find the old bastard, lock him in a room or something. Say, Benetsee, I got this wine out here, you tell me stories that I like, you get some. But not till I really like them damn stories.

I got no talent for being a bastard, torture a harmless old man. Leave that to Bucky Dassault, other helpful bastards. The Sheriff's such a fool, he think Benetsee's one too.

I got to find that old man, ask him, please, here, take this wine but tell me what you know. I won't tell anyone else, I tell you before God (who is deaf, or was when my wife died) but I need to know.

Coyotes sing now, they make the hairs on the back of my neck stand up, there. Real straight.

Du Pré looked down on some fine big country. He thought about the skreeking Red River carts, the people, the buffalo driven into stout log pens to be killed at leisure, the meat sliced off their bones in sheets a quarter-inch thick, hung on willow racks over fires, baled up and tied with sinew, bundles stacked in the carts and then every-body turned around and went back north.

At night the fiddles came out, the people danced, the men smoked and played cards on a blanket.

They smoked that meat right down there, went round the mountains to the east, played the fiddle right down there, made babies, longed for home, the priest.

The Black Robes, they come, have incense, golden kingdoms up above. But what good are priests, anyway, won't make medicine help you to steal more horses? Send smallpox to them damn Blackfeet and Sioux. Protestants even sorrier, not even incense, they get called Short Robes.

So I find that old man, see if maybe he tell me something.

'Sides I miss him, he comes from another time, like them buffalo hunters, like my grandfathers.

Red River.

❖ CHAPTER 21 ❖

Old Benetsee was at his shack, carving pipes from the red, close-grained stone quarried for five thousand years over near Pipestone Pass. He would fit them with a willow stem, hang a few chicken feathers on them, spread them on a blanket and wait for shoals of tourists.

Benetsee's hands shook quite a bit, but when he bent to dig another bit of red stone out of the deepening bowl they didn't.

"Ho Benetsee," said Du Pré. He had a jug of cheap white wine in a paper sack. He felt like a turd.

The old man looked up and nodded.

"I been expecting you," he said. "How are all your beautiful women; Jacqueline, Maria, that nice Madelaine?"

"Fine," said Gabriel. "They ask about you some. Wonder if you all right, hope things go well for you."

"I got no pretty women," said Benetsee. He seemed relieved about it. "If I had one now I'd be doing too well. Better this way, I don't have to wash so much."

Scritch scritch on the pipe.

Fifty centuries of that sound. Make that a couple million years. Some old fart going scritch scritch on the whatever, punctuate his teasings of a younger fool. Lot of men, stand where I am now. This dust is full of them.

"You hear about I find these three skulls where there should be only two?"

Scritch scritch nod.

"Well," said Du Pré, "what about that, you know?"

Benetsee looked up, head cocked, eye bright as a bird's.

"Coyote tell me much," said Benetsee, "but it very hard pick out just what he is saying, how much he is playing with me."

Tell me about it, thought Du Pré.

Benetsee dug at the pipe bowl. He seemed to have forgotten that Du Pré was standing there.

"You want some wine?" said Du Pré. Now maybe you remember me.

"Good morning to drink wine," said Benetsee, putting down his pipe, the little black awl with the deerskin wrapping the end held in the palm.

Du Pré handed Benetsee the jug.

The old man took a long pull of the gassy cheap wine. He belched and handed the jug back to Du Pré. A whiff of the wine hit Du Pré's nose, his mouth ran water, he felt like throwing up.

I am drinking too much whiskey these days, Du Pré

thought, I know better but when I drink a lot of it I don't grind my teeth in my sleep so much.

"Have some wine, good morning for it," said Benetsee. He looked far away, up to the Wolf Mountains. Little sharp face, Du Pré thought of the shrew's skull in the coyote scat. In his pocket.

Du Pré choked down some. Jesus, like drinking bubble gum.

"Whew," said Du Pré, "you much man, drink that."

"Poor man drink that," said Benetsee. He looked at his fingernails, rimmed in black, clawed old hands, the veins and tendons seen easily through the transparent skin.

"So what you want to know?" said Benetsee. "I don't know too much. Coyote knows a lot, but me, not too much."

Du Pré felt the warm bloom of the wine in his stomach. A nice warm peaceful feeling, he sat down next to the old man, put his elbows on his knees, rolled a cigarette. Gave it to him, rolled another for himself, lit both.

"Brings me wine, brings me tobacco," said Benetsee. "Hard to find a respectful young man these days."

"The Headless Man," said Du Pré, "how did his head get up in the mountains, in a place a goat wouldn't have, next to a wrecked plane fell down so long ago they think maybe it just flew to heaven."

Benetsee reached for the jug. *Glug glug glug.*

"Well," said Benetsee, "somebody very angry, of course. So you kill someone, you put the head and hands with some other bones, let the magpies and coyotes and skunks stir them. So maybe no one will know, what happened."

"I got that," said Du Pré.

"How long your parents been dead now, Gabriel," said Benetsee. "A bad day, that one."

Very bad day. Papa drunk and Mama deaf, car stall on a railroad crossing, didn't find a piece of either of them big enough to call Mama, Papa. Closed coffins at the funeral, coffins very light to carry, too.

Good people. Du Pré had loved them both. Killed while Du Pré was in basic training, Fort Ord. Du Pré, eighteen, only child. His mother always shamed she couldn't have more babies, like a good Métis woman.

"You know," said Benetsee, "most times there is a killing, there is a pretty woman in it somewhere, you know?"

Du Pré thought. His mama? Jesus, no, the two of them loved each other, make a pass at either, whoever, they wouldn't even notice.

"What the hell you mean?" said Du Pré.

But the old man had picked up the pipestone again.

Scritch scritch.

✤ CHAPTER 22 ✤

I tell you, Madelaine, I like to strangle that old bastard," said Du Pré. Diddle me out of that wine, leave me more confused than a newspaper.

"Well," said Madelaine, "you men get crazy, kill each other over us, you know. But you right, I don't see where he's pointing."

Early morning, her kids were stirring, time to get ready for school.

Du Pré rolled on his side, held her sweet warmth close.

71

"Got to cook them breakfast, see about their clothes," said Madelaine. "Old Benetsee, he talk to me, maybe?"

"Don't know."

Madelaine nuzzled his neck.

"Long time ago," said Madelaine. "Who around then? That old priest, Father Leblanc?"

Du Pré remembered. Father Leblanc had retired long ago, moved back up north to Canada, the fathers had a rest home there.

Red River.

Madelaine got up, Du Pré slept till the door banged to for the last time. He heard the grind of the school bus going off. Madelaine had four kids, they left Du Pré alone, he left them alone. But the oldest boy was needing a man to learn from.

I don't know what to do for my daughters, thought I at least would not have to not understand a son, too. Jesus, she got three more of them. Life, it get you every time.

Du Pré dressed, walked to the kitchen, carrying his boots. Madelaine dished him up some scrambled eggs, salsa, a couple slices of her good bread with chokecherry jam.

Du Pré ate.

"I got some fence to fix," he said, "check my place out." My few cows, horses, brushed-up little creek. I fix it up, work hard, lose more money.

He drove home. Maria was gone, off to school, bad-ass girl on the Honor Roll. People she hung around with probably couldn't read well enough to see her name, she's safe.

What about all this.

Du Pré filled a pocket of his down vest with fencing staples, took a fencing tool, a shovel, a topper's ax.

When he heaved against the rusty barbwire gate the top

72

strand broke, so he had to go back and pull a coil of wire off the spool. He fixed the gate, shut it, began to slowly walk the fence. Do a mile or so today, then more sometime. If his cattle got out they would be hazed back by the neighbors. No bitching, no cattleman needs the brand inspector pissed off at him.

Du Pré topped a little rise, looked down, saw four of his neighbor's steers at rest in his pasture. They got up when they saw him, trotted back home. Du Pré followed them to the downed fence. A post had rotted off, a cow had leaned against it until it snapped and the fence went down. Lots of tracks both ways.

I'd better fix this fence, here. Not too good a neighbor, me.

Du Pré cut a new post from a dead juniper, dug out a shallow hole, set and tamped the post. He stapled the wires back on.

The four steers looked glumly at him from the neighbor's pasture.

Spoilsport.

Du Pré saw his horses, one was limping. He hadn't worked his stock, they looked at him and trotted off, all but the one who was hurt in the foot.

"Tch tch," Du Pré clucked, coming up to the gelding. The oldest one, twenty years, gentle old fellow.

Du Pré patted the horse's neck. He lifted the left front hoof, saw the bad split.

Du Pré slipped his belt off, put it round the horse's neck, led him back to the little tumbledown barn. Got to fix these hinges, too, whole place is slumped and tired.

Us Du Pré, we been here a while.

Du Pré found the old inner tube, the rope, the Epsom salts. He went to the house, made up a batch of warm water, poured in the salts. He carried the kettle back out to

73

the barn and slipped the inner tube over the horse's leg, tied it up, rope over the horse's withers. Poured in the warm drawing water, the horse danced a little at the strange feeling.

"Hohoho," said Du Pré. The horse stood, liking the warmth on his sore hoof and leg.

Du Pré left him there, went to the house for lunch.

He found a can of sardines, can of tomatoes. What the West was built on, cowboys ate and drank these. Piles of rusty cans at every good place to stop and have lunch. Ghost meals.

Du Pré went to the living room, cluttered with the magazines Maria brought home, but clean. He looked at the pictures on the mantel. Catfoot and Maman. Maria. Jacqueline, big smile, first baby, boy of course, Gabriel, of course.

Du Pré at a fiddlers' contest, first place, Du Pré half-drunk in the picture, little cheap trophy in his hand.

Picture of his father's sister, Aunt Pauline, with one of her husbands.

Aunty Pauline, blond, brown-eyed, good-looking woman. Trouble woman, she'd had three husbands.

Aunty Pauline, used to ride trick horses in the rodeo.

She'd be maybe sixty now? Du Pré hadn't seen her in more than twenty years.

Aunty Pauline.

Who Mama wouldn't speak of after that one time.

Du Pré didn't know what had happened. Long time ago.

Where was Aunty Pauline now?

Red River.

✤ CHAPTER 23 ✤

Du Pré was flicking his eyes over the brands, the cattle bawled in the chute. Funny job he had, no one needed him, then they opened the newspaper, saw prices up, or the banker didn't want to extend the note and they all wanted him right now. He'd be working till midnight tonight, for sure.

Pretty dull, too. While I'm here, somebody within twenty miles is losing cattle. The thieves pay attention to the market price, too.

"Du Pré! DU PRÉ!" the rancher yelling, right in Du Pré's ear.

Du Pré didn't take his eyes off the stock.

"All hell broke loose up to that rich folks' place," said the rancher, "the Sheriff's been shot dead."

"What?" Du Pré took his eyes off the stock.

"I got a scanner," said the rancher. "Deputies screaming, say the Sheriff's dead on the lawn and people are shooting from the house."

Du Pré looked back at the stock, found his place. Brands all OK. So what's this? Shit.

"Don't you need to get over there?"

"No," said Du Pré. "I need to see this stock loaded, then I got to go over to Koch's to see about theirs. There's nothing I can do about . . . all that crap at Fascelis'." Dumb bastard, that Sheriff.

75

So they loaded the cattle, Du Pré signed off, got in his car, cursed a while, turned on the radio.

"DUPREE DUPREE DUPREE GOD DAMN IT COME IN DUPREE DUPREE!" said the dispatcher, sounding hoarse.

"Yes," said Du Pré, very quietly.

"DUPREE!"

"Yes," said Du Pré, "it's me. And the answer is no."

"Get over to the Fascellis right away, the guy shooting says he will come out but he wants you there, wants to walk out with you. Won't have anybody else. MOVE IT."

Shit. SHIT.

"No," said Du Pré. "I don't do that, no."

The dispatcher started screaming, so Du Pré switched off his radio. Rolled a cigarette. Smoked it. Spat out the window.

He switched the radio back on.

"What about the Sheriff, now?"

"DU PREE, he's dead on the damn lawn. Look, I am sorry I yelled at you. Please go over there before somebody else gets killed. Please."

"OK." SHIT SHIT SHIT.

Du Pré thought maybe he'd drive over to Benetsee's hideout, stay drunk for a week. What's this all about, now? Huh?

He drove toward Fascelli's, the Crossed Eyes Ranch. I look at cow asses, I don't have to do this I don't have to do this.

But I do.

Shit. SHIT.

He could see the house, spotlighted. A helicopter circled over it.

The Sheriff was on his back on the lawn, his head all bloody. He was wearing a bulletproof vest.

Seven deputies were crouched around, some Highway Patrolmen, lots of assault rifles and shotguns.

"Now, what?" said Du Pré. He had decided to address this to a silver-haired Highway Patrolman who looked so disgusted he likely had a fair idea of what was really going on. Du Pré guessed.

"You Du Pré," said the HP. He had Scott Parsons on a nameplate above his left shirt pocket.

"Yes," said Du Pré.

"Well," said Parsons, "this guy keeps screaming that he won't come out unless you go in, he didn't shoot the Sheriff, and he also feels that we are a bunch of fucking assholes."

"No shit," said Du Pré.

"He's probably right on all counts," said Parsons.

"How many other people in there?"

"I don't know," said Parsons. "When I got here things were about like they are."

"OK," said Du Pré, "I go talk to him." He walked out across the lawn, hollering "BART BART! It's DU PRÉ." He walked out into the lights, holding his hands away from his sides.

"That is you, Du Pré," said Fascelli.

"I don't got a gun," said Du Pré. "Where's your sister, the maids and all?"

"In the swimming pool," said Bart. "It's empty. When these idiot assholes started shooting I had them get in there. I got in there, too. Where do they find these people, anyway?"

Du Pré looked down at the Sheriff. His face was gone. So he'd been shot in the *back* of the head.

"OK," said Du Pré, "I am coming up to the front door and I am arresting you and I am taking you to the jail. We do it fast, OK?"

"Sure," said Fascelli.

Du Pré went to the big ornate carved front door, it opened, Bart stepped out. Du Pré took his arm.

"I don't got no handcuffs," said Du Pré, "but we play I do."

"Hi, Mom," said Fascelli, smiling out at the floodlights. He clasped his hands behind his back while Du Pré pretended to clap cuffs on his wrists.

Du Pré and his prisoner walked out to the silver-haired Highway Patrolman.

"I arrest him," said Du Pré, "you drive us to the jail, huh?"

"You read him his rights?" said Parsons.

"Oh, yes, officer," said Fascelli.

Du Pré and Fascelli got in the back of the car. Du Pré left the door open.

"You got some handcuffs I can borrow," said Du Pré. "He ought to be wearing them we get to the jail."

Parsons unsnapped the case on his belt, unlocked the cuffs, and handed them to Du Pré.

"You don't have to do that," said Fascelli. "I won't give you any trouble."

"Look," said Du Pré, "you better be wearing these when we get there, these fools think you half-escaped or something." He looked at the shot-up house, the milling deputies, all armed, all looking very lost.

He snapped the cuffs on Bart's wrists.

Parsons drove fast all the way to Cooper.

The last sight Du Pré had of the scene of the siege was of four people standing around the body of the Sheriff.

But that Sheriff, he wasn't ever going to get up.

✤ CHAPTER 24 ✤

D u Pré," said Madelaine, "you been having a rough time lately. Maybe you better go see Father Van Den Heuvel."

"I need to build up my sins," said Du Pré. "Big stack of them so that God handles this personally."

Madelaine threw up her hands. All this means, Du Pré, he has to blaspheme.

"So what did Foosli tell you?"

"He said he's inside the house, having drinks with his sister, the Sheriff is suddenly on the lawn with a bullhorn yelling for Bart to come out with his hands up. So he goes to the window, wondering who is playing this joke on him, and there is this shot, hits the Sheriff right in the back of the head, comes from behind the fence and the hedge. The other deputies go crazy, they shoot for a while or scream into the radio for a while, and Bart tells everybody in the house, get into the swimming pool—they got one there, middle of the house, cause they won't get shot there. They get in it."

Madelaine poured some more coffee for Du Pré.

"So then Bart say he shoot a few times over their heads, say he won't surrender to no one but me. 'They are stupid and crazy,' said Bart to me, 'so I know you at least.' He trusts me. I don't blame him, not wanting come out in front of them deputies."

"But who shoot the Sheriff?" said Madelaine.

79

Du Pré thought that he knew but he also thought he didn't give a rusty shit at this point. Also he wasn't going to tell anyone he damn well knew old Booger Tom had done it, see if he could get the cops so riled they kill everyone in the house.

"Whew," said Madelaine. "What the Sheriff going to arrest him for, anyway?"

"I don't know," said Du Pré.

"This very mysterious."

"This very stupid, what this is, I think. You seen Maria?"

"At the grocery store."

Du Pré nodded. "I better go out to the house, see if she is there, tell her I love her, case she's forgot."

"Du Pré," said Madelaine, "why don't you tell me you love me, case I forgot."

They held each other.

Du Pré went out, started up his old car, shifted into reverse.

Madelaine came after him.

"Du Pré," she said, "you got a dirty temper, you keep it close for me and Maria and Jacqueline and all. You don't got a mean bone in your body but you sure got lots of mad ones. Mad bones break pretty easy. All them cops, they are upset. One of them get shot dead, the others go crazy."

Du Pré nodded.

"Give my love to Maria," said Madelaine.

They all really take care of me, Du Pré thought. Now what I do for them? Really?

Maria was in the kitchen, cooking a goose. She'd washed the colored crap out of her hair and didn't have any makeup on. She had enormous black eyes, like her mama. She moved like her mama. Du Pré suddenly went very sad.

80

"Lots of calls on the phone, I told everybody you went to the dog races, Spokane," said Maria. She grinned.

Du Pré smiled. Maybe he would go to Spokane, hide out.

"Some lawyer for Fascelli called, wants you to call him. He's staying in Cooper, the little motel."

Du Pré grunted. Fascelli, he wasn't guilty of anything but a busted life, got to be cold as the moon. Back of the head, the slug that got the Sheriff. Booger Tom? Could the old fart still see that well? Or did one of the deputies get the twitch, all the wide world to hit and the bullet gets the Sheriff?

"I'm the head of the Honor Roll again," said Maria. "So I thought today, this morning, I'd wash my face and be a good little Catholic girl again."

Du Pré nodded. He'd never been fooled, but he had held his breath a few times.

"Also I don't think you need to talk to Bucky Dassault again. You got plenty on your plate, Papa. I won't let you down."

"You never have let me down, Maria," said Du Pré. "Maybe I let you down sometimes. I don't know what to do, you know."

"No, you love me good. You proud of me, proud of Jacqueline."

"Yes."

"Can I help you," Maria said, "I would, too."

Du Pré hugged her. Maria gave him a sunny wide smile.

Du Pré drove off to Cooper, see this attorney. Probably some expensive attorney from New York or something. Lizard briefcase. Manicure.

Platform shoes.

✤ CHAPTER 25 ✤

"This *farce*," said the attorney, "confirms what I always believed to be the case of Montana."

Young guy, lots of money, three-piece suit fit him so well he seemed to flow one place to another, like water. Long thin dark face. Deep, precise voice.

Probably never been on a dirt road before in his life.

"They don't do things like this, Dee-troyt?" said Du Pré. He sipped his coffee.

The lawyer regarded his with loathing, like it had dripped out of a sick bull.

"Did you know," said the attorney, "that Mr. Fascelli was holding the squadrons of the law at bay with a *starter pistol?* That there wasn't a live round of ammunition in the house, for obvious reasons. Barbara Fascelli is at the Betty Ford Center for the nth time. Bart will be out on bond this very day, and I will take him to a quiet place in Michigan. The maids left in a body, the masseur left with the hairdresser, the refrigerator is full of rotting caviar, and there is no case whatever. Thank you, by the way, for saving the life of my client. Each time one or another Fascelli dies there is a protracted struggle over the remaining millions. The money is excellent, but the work squalid."

Du Pré had never met a creature like this attorney, Foote. He thought about it. Probably didn't matter who got elected president, this was one of them as ran the country. Quietly.

"What do you think of all this?" said Foote, leaning forward. He seemed genuinely interested in Du Pré's thoughts.

"I don't know," said Du Pré. "I kind of like Bart. But he got not one chance in life he don't run away, take nothing of that damn money, spend his days washing dishes or something. He's not a bad guy, but he is in a very bad place."

"No," said Foote, "he is not a bad guy, and that is that."

"But who shot the Sheriff?" said Du Pré.

"One of the deputies, probably," said Foote. "I have yet to see the autopsy and ballistics report, but I would expect one or another of his faithful sidekicks misfired while loading one or another of the assault rifles."

Booger Tom probably can't see that well anyway, thought Du Pré, and I don't *care*.

"One thing I still don't know," said Du Pré. "What was the Sheriff going to arrest Bart for?"

"Um," said Foote, "you really don't know? He was going to arrest Bart for murdering his brother, Gianni, who disappeared nearly thirty years ago."

Du Pré nodded. "So the teeth match up?"

"Maybe they do, maybe they don't," said Foote. "Nothing back from the state lab. The Sheriff, mind you—he must have been pretty drunk—didn't even have a *warrant*."

Du Pré looked up, laughed. "You're shitting me."

"I am not. I suppose he spent a couple pleasant days at the jug, watching Clint Eastwood movies over and over. Like I said, I had always suspected Montana was a place chockful of people too stupid to walk downhill, which is where civilization is, if you are at all interested."

Du Pré nodded. He wasn't interested in civilization.

"Anyway," said Foote, "I bear thanks to you from Bart, who feels you probably saved his life. So do I."

83

Du Pré shrugged.

"Bart only understands giving money away to express gratitude. He is astute enough to realize that you do not need or want money, and he fervently wishes that he was the same. But he did think that an offer to send your daughter to any school she can get into, all expenses, all travel, everything, contingent upon her making good grades—he is not prepared to render another human being as worthless as he feels himself to be—might possibly not be offensive to you."

Du Pré's eyebrows shot up. He suddenly realized that Maria would have her dream, if she wanted it, and she might not know even that it was her dream. She wanted the best, would work hard for it.

Now, Du Pré, he thought, don't get the swelled head.

"Well," said Du Pré, "it's fine with me, but my opinion, it don't mean shit, really, so he would have to talk to my daughter."

Foote's eyes shot up. Sideways. He tipped his chair back and laughed.

"She is a minor, Mr. Du Pré," said Foote, "so your blessing is vital. I am to take it she is an independent girl."

"Her own damn country, she is," said Du Pré.

"Well," said Foote, "I have time enough to make the offer to her in person, if we can find her. Prior to taking Bart back East. I have a Learjet due in at five."

Du Pré shook his head. Bart was a nice man, should do something, anything, not die screaming in some alky hospital.

Du Pré drove Foote to the high school in Cooper, fetched Maria out of class, stuck her in the car with the young attorney, took a walk in the gray light so he didn't screw things up by hovering.

He came back in fifteen minutes, to find Foote and

Maria sitting on the dented hood of his old police cruiser. They were laughing.

Foote was smoking a long thin cheroot.

Maria was grinning like a mule eating chitlins.

Foote offered Du Pré a cigar.

Du Pré smoked it reverently. It was the best tobacco he had ever had.

Before Maria went back into the school, she kissed her father.

"See what happen," she said, "to a daughter of a good Métis man?"

Du Pré drove Foote to the courthouse.

They shook hands.

Foote's eyes crinkled with a kindly intelligence. He offered his hand again.

"That's for me," said Foote. "Bart's the only decent one of the bunch. Thanks. He deserves some help, not the twaddle they will give him at the place where I am taking him."

"He come back?" said Du Pré.

"Probably," said Foote.

"He ought to," said Du Pré.

"I think so too."

Du Pré drove off, wondering about a lot of things.

✤ CHAPTER 26 ✤

I ain't so smart but I'll do my best," said the acting sheriff, Benny Klein, former long-haul trucker and present little rancher. "I can't believe old Sheriff Johnson didn't have no warrant."

I can, thought Du Pré, that one dumb bastard. This Benny, he will do a pretty good job, if he don't die of terror when he has to speak to Kiwanis or something.

"So what do you think of all this, Du Pré?"

Benny held a report that said that the teeth could well have come from the jaw of Gianni Fascelli, or someone like him had those same holes in those same teeth. Lots of people got holes in those two teeth, nothing exclusive about it.

Du Pré shrugged.

"I got to go, inspect some cattle," he said. "I don't want any more of this mess. I am a simple cow-ass expert. I check to see them cows branded outside, not inside, them hides, I sign off. I have work to do on my one-horse ranch. I got two daughters. I am not a detective. Good thing, too. For everybody."

Klein nodded. It was about three in the afternoon. Lawyer Foote and a vodka-swilling Bart Fascelli had taken off in a prop plane, they would catch the Learjet in Miles City, a whole week ago.

Good luck to him, thought Du Pré, that lawyer, he don't need luck, he make his own.

Maria was bringing home six, eight library books a day and she was staying up till four in the morning reading them.

I got one married off, thought Du Pré, making babies and loving them and me, the other going to get a Nobel Prize in something, soon as she figure out what. Now I got to worry about Madelaine's four.

I got to take that oldest boy hunting, explain to him about rubbers.

The fire alarm sounded, Du Pré and Klein looked at each other. The county fire department was whoever happened to be in hearing of the alarm and near to the old fire truck, which had been bought in 1948 and used a lot. It was a pretty thing, faded red and lots of brass and gauges, but it wasn't much at putting out fires, which had mostly burned completely out before the truck lumbered up and the crew remembered just exactly how to hook up the hoses.

Du Pré and the Sheriff walked outside, looked up toward the Bench. There was a giant column of black smoke coming from the very place the Fascellis' huge ugly fat wet house was.

"Shit," said acting Sheriff Klein. He jumped in his car and drove off, without his hat. Du Pré followed him. The fire truck would get there by and by, in time to damp down the ashes.

God, Du Pré thought, looking at the blazing house. Flames were shooting a hundred feet in the air, glass was shattering, and the roof and some of the walls had already fallen in. You couldn't get closer than a couple hundred feet.

Booger Tom was sitting on the fence, working on a fifth of whiskey like he meant it.

"How the hell the fire start?" said the Sheriff to Booger Tom.

"Oh, that," said Booger Tom. "Well, Mr. Bart wrote me a letter, said he'd canceled the insurance, and to burn the place down. Sent five hundred bucks to buy gasoline and diesel fuel—told me to make sure—said he wasn't defrauding anyone and he would goddamned well burn down his own house if he wanted to."

"So I soaked the place down, opened the windows, tossed in a match, and there she is. Hah." *Glug glug.*

Du Pré laughed so hard he doubled up.

The new sheriff scratched his head.

"Well," he said, "people burn down old barns all the time. You get a burning permit?"

"No," said Booger Tom. "Piss on your damn burning permit."

"I'll have to write you a ticket," said Sheriff Klein.

Booger Tom nodded graciously. "Want a drink?" he said, offering the bottle to Klein.

"No," said the Sheriff, "I better not. I seem to remember that the fine is fifteen dollars or something. Just come in to the courthouse when you have a mind to."

Booger Tom nodded.

There was a towering column of flame rising up in the exact center of the burning house.

"That's the three hundred gallons of diesel in the swimming pool, said Booger Tom. "I thought of that my own self. *Belch.*"

The Sheriff left, Du Pré watched the fire.

"Hey, Du Pré," said Booger Tom, "there's a little note here for you from Fascelli."

Du Pré held it out at arm's length, squinted.

"Dear Du Pré"—the handwriting was pretty shaky and loopy, so Bart wasn't feeling so good when he wrote it—"I am coming back and when I do I am going to raise the cows myself, live in a sheepwagon, and make Booger Tom the foreman and me the hand. I promise, Bart."

"Hey, Tom," said Du Pré, "you know Fascelli says he is going to come back, make you the foreman, himself the hand?"

"Yup," said Booger Tom.

"What you think of that?"

"Well," said Booger Tom, "I think that if Mr. Bart will learn how to shovel shit and like it, or at least say that he does, he might do all right."

Du Pré nodded.

There was a God, maybe, time to time.

✦ CHAPTER 27 ✦

Benetsee motioned to Du Pré. I got to pee. The old man clambered out, stood swaying, pissed. It was dark out, cold with frost.

They were supposed to be hunting deer.

Which meant that maybe Du Pré would shoot a deer for the old man, but the drunken old fart's gun was going to stay locked in the trunk of the car. Argue all you want, old man, the answer is no.

"The hunter dream the deer and the deer come," said Benetsee.

"Shape you in, I don't want to see what you dream come at all," said Du Pré. The car smelled like the drunk tank. Benetsee belched, adding a little more to the stench.

"Park here," said Benetsee. Du Pré parked where he was

going to park anyway. The brush below hid a path deer used. Every day. Morning and evening.

It was a half hour or so till the light would begin to rise. Du Pré got his rifle from the trunk, came back to the warm seat in the wine fug.

He rolled a cigarette, handed it to Benetsee. The old man dug in his dirty jacket for matches, found some, lit it. Du Pré rolled himself another.

"So," said Benetsee. He took a pinch of tobacco, rolled down his window, muttered for a moment, dropped the wad to the ground.

An offering.

They sat, smoking.

Du Pré poured himself some coffee. He sipped it. The purls of steam rose and stuck to the windshield.

"Too much excitement lately," said Benetsee, "but I think things calm some now. People ought to go out, sit, wait for deer more. It is restful."

Smoke. Belch.

"Wonder who shot that fool Sheriff," said Du Pré. The FBI had finally been called in on some bullshit pretext, they were being snotty to everyone. The bullet that had gone through the Sheriff's head had gone right on into the house and maybe out the other side and maybe not. Anyway, now the house was a sump of smelly ashes. Who knows?

Du Pré had seen the report on the Sheriff. Death instantaneous. Since everybody started in firing like fools the moment after the Sheriff went splat on his back it was extremely hard to find out where anybody thought the first shot had come from.

What with everything, it was even impossible for the FBI to frame anybody, like they usually did.

Du Pré was finding the whole thing hilarious. The FBI

had interviewed all four of the Sheriff's deputies who had been crouched there in backup, and who had fired every round they had for the rifles within a couple minutes of the Sheriff's rapid shuffle off this here mortal coil.

The Highway Patrolmen had arrived a little later, and they hadn't fired a shot among them.

Du Pré never took a gun out of his car.

Booger Tom was not likely to confess in a fit of remorse, on account of Booger Tom was not the type to feel such a furrin emotion.

Talk all they want, them FBI, not much good, that.

There was a rattle of scree, flat little rocks racketing down a slide of stone. Something there had loosened them.

The trail led across the scree to the trail Du Pré would watch just as soon as it got light.

Du Pré got out, racked a shell into the chamber, took the caps off the lenses of the sight. The scope was light-gathering, and he could see well enough if the deer wasn't behind a bush. It would be another half hour before he could see a deer behind branches well.

Du Pré swung the rifle, looked out at the spot on the trail he'd shot maybe two dozen deer on in his life. Some even in season. In Montana, one out of five deer shot was taken legally. Since the cattle business in Montana had collapsed, the ranchers weren't even killing deer wholesale to keep them off the grass and out of the haystacks, so there were lots more deer now than when Du Pré was a boy.

Du Pré saw a nice six-point buck, swung the scope back, put the post and crosshair on the spot where the spine joined the skull.

POWWWWW . . . and the echoes, back and forth, back and forth.

The deer was flopping, just a little. Good place to aim for, since either the animal dropped in its tracks or Du Pré missed clean. He hurried down to the deer and slit its throat to drain it. If he shot the deer in the chest he didn't have to do that, but it messed up the ribs and organs, and the liver was the best part.

Du Pré walked back up to the car, jacking the shells out of the rifle. He put the rifle in the trunk and walked back, dragged the deer to a spot where it lay downhill, watched the bright blood plume from the throat.

Blood steamed on the stones.

Du Pré ringed the anus, tied it off, slit the deer open, jammed his hands into the chest cavity and grabbed hold of the windpipe, esophagus, and heart. He heaved. The viscera came free.

He pulled a plastic bag from his pocket, shook it open, set it beside the guts. He cut out the heart and liver, dropped them into the sack, reached into the abdomen and carved the kidneys out from their wads of backfat. He closed the bloody sack and stuck it in the game pouch of his coat.

Du Pré dragged the deer up to the car, his feet sometimes slipping on the wet stones. It was hard work, the animal weighed closer to three hundred pounds than two. Du Pré was running sweat by the time he had it on the ground behind the car.

He opened the trunk and heaved the deer in. He propped the trunk open so that the air would cool the carcass. He stuck sticks in the chest cavity to keep it open, cool that meat.

"Where's your tag?" said Du Pré to Benetsee.

"No," said Benetsee. He had some more wine.

Du Pré tagged the deer with his own tag.

This old fart got nerve.

I owe him one.

✤ CHAPTER 28 ✤

Got you good, didn't he?" said Madelaine. She was
stuffing Du Pré's bloody clothes into her washing
machine.

"No," said Du Pré. "I expected it."

"He's some old fart, eh?" she said, adding detergent to
the wash.

Du Pré was rosining his bow, getting ready to fiddle for
a ribbon. Blue. My favorite color.

Maria was coming to hear Du Pré fiddle, and Jacqueline,
too. He had given Jacqueline money for a babysitter, so she
and Raymond could have a little time away from the babies. Raymond worked like three men to keep them all,
fine young man, perhaps in time he could fall into something paid better than jackknife carpentry, plumbing, the
feed mill.

Du Pré heard the door. Maria, laughing, and so was
Madelaine, both very gay. Like they had some secret, a
happy one.

"Hey, Du Pré," Madelaine called. "Let go yourself,
come out here, see how your women love you."

I know my women love me, thought Du Pré, now what
is this?

The two women smiled at him. Jacqueline had come
from somewhere and she, too, sat on the couch. Big white
box on the coffee table, blue ribbon, little card in an
envelope.

Du Pré raised an eyebrow. "Now what's this?

"So open it, see," said Jacqueline. All three giggled.

Du Pré took the little card out. To our good Métis man, love.

Du Pré opened the ribbon knots, let the blue ribbon fall to the table, fold it up, use it again, hardly wrinkled.

Tissue paper.

Du Pré folded it back. A vest on top, soft white leather, all worked with quills in patterns, hummingbirds and suns and teepees, animals. Beautiful. The quills were all dyed with the old dyes, from sunflowers, salmonberries, choke-cherry root, he hadn't seen those dyes in many years.

A soft cream silk shirt, full sleeves, tight cuffs.

Gaiters of soft white deerskin, quilled with beaver tails, the Pole Star and Big Dipper. Compasses.

A red velvet sash with black beads.

Moccasins with turquoise and yellow and red and black beadwork. Nez Percé that.

A little round Red River hat, soft black felt, with a beaded band and a hard narrow brim.

A bright turquoise silk scarf.

"My my," said Du Pré. "This is too fine stuff for me."

"We made the stuff from what we could see in that old picture of your great-grandfather," said Jacqueline. "Maria found them dyes, in a book, no one living we know knows them."

"So, you happy?" said Madelaine.

Du Pré's throat choked up. Such good people, his women. All this must have taken many hours.

He lifted the vest, looked at the tiny careful stitchings.

"My, my," he said, slipping it on, fit perfectly over his old stained blue work shirt.

"Papa," said Maria, "you put it all on, not one thing at a time."

94

Du Pré dressed in the bedroom, all the finery. He looked at himself in the big mirror, the dark skin, straight black Indian hair, black mustache. A Métis man, got a fiddle and a pipe.

"We take this fine-looking man to the fiddling contest," said Madelaine. She beamed at Du Pré.

I got me some beautiful women, I'm very lucky.

They all piled into Du Pré's old cruiser, went off to the old Toussaint Bar. It had another name many years ago but someone didn't like it and blew the sign off with a shotgun one very-drunk-out Saturday night. So it was the Toussaint Bar, no sign.

Du Pré was embarrassed when he walked through the door, he hoped he wouldn't have to shove anybody's teeth down his throat for insulting the beautiful handiwork of his women.

People whistled. A couple old grandmothers came to him and one got right down on the floor to look at the fine beaded moccasins. The other fingered the sash.

They rattled at Madelaine in Coyote French, waved their hands and beamed, their store-bought teeth too blue-white.

The fiddle contest began, and Du Pré blew everybody's hats in the creek. He pinned the blue ribbon to his Red River hat. He looked down at his moccasins, up at his women. He beamed.

He played a tune about the sounds the axles of the carts made when the people came down here to hunt the buffalo, make winter meat, do the hard dirty bloody work, sing while they did it. Get everybody set for that long cold Northern winter. Black ravens on white earth. Wolves howling in the river bottoms. The men wandering far on their long woodland snowshoes, Cree snowshoes, get those furs, buy calico and guns, kettles and rum, beads and

medicine, brass tacks for the rifle stocks, salt and tea, dried
fruit, maybe coffee.

"Good, Du Pré" cried the grandmothers, swaying.

Red River.

✤ C H A P T E R   2 9 ✤

Thanksgiving. Du Pré and the priest went to fetch Benetsee. Back at Du Pré's house, three women, one kitchen.
Jesus.

Du Pré parked out on the road by Benetsee's shack, saw
the dirty white plume of the smoke from his fire, felt the
acid bite of it in his nostrils, on his tongue.

Du Pré and the priest trudged to Benetsee's door, Du Pré
tapped twice, turned the latch, let go when the old man
swung the door open. A warm fetor poured out, stale food,
stale wine, old man, tobacco, wet dogs. The two old dogs,
heelers, left over from Benetsee's days in a sheepwagon,
tending the woollies. They were nearly blind and so stiff
they rocked from side to side when they walked. Wheezy
woofs. Honor satisfied, they staggered back to bed beside
the stove.

"Good day," said Benetsee. The old man was sober,
clear-eyed, had combed his shock of white hair, black eyes
glittered in his brown face. He'd dressed up, old necktie
even, gravy stains and greasy spots. Mostly clean shirt. He
shrugged into an old army greatcoat, picked up a bundle
of brain-tanned deerhide.

"Good you come for me," he said, "long walk."

Du Pré looked out into the yard, two old trucks up on blocks, under the snow.

They walked to the car, the clumsy priest nearly fell.

Way things going, thought Du Pré, everybody have to stay at my house. I got plenty of blankets, lots of floors.

Nice soft floors, though.

"How have you been, Benetsee," said the priest. "I think of you often."

Benetsee thought for a moment. "Old," he said, "I been old."

They all laughed, got in Du Pré's car.

Sush sush sush went the tires in the deep snow. County plows wouldn't be out for a while, maybe not till tomorrow. Du Pré remembered riding in them with Catfoot, his father cursing and shifting gears. The trucks were old, Catfoot slammed them into drifted snow so hard sometimes the trucks slowed and stopped, went sideways.

Then the wind would put the snow back.

Catfoot got called out on bad nights, he had a couple old trucks and plows, not too much good, but anything helped when the blizzards came. Catfoot, the little rancher, brand inspector, roadman for the county, combiner of grain, good hand at poker. Did everything. Had to.

Du Pré shifted in his seat. His ass itched.

"Your women very kind," said Benetsee. "I don't hear from my sons and daughters any more."

Too much trouble to them, thought Du Pré, that's very sad. He thought more. Too much trouble to *me*, thinking about the deer hanging in Benetsee's meathouse with Du Pré's tag on its leg.

Old fart. Good old man, knows things.

Du Pré turned into the drive to his house. The snow and wind had erased his tracks. Raymond's pickup was there now, he'd been out fixing someone's plumbing. Hard-working man.

They struggled through the snow to the house. Du Pré walked behind, ready to grab the clumsy priest or the old man, but they made it to the door all right. The priest sort of fell into the house.

The house was hot and steamy from all the people sweating, the cooking, the old Peerless woodstove hot and covered in dishes.

Much laughter, whiskey and lemon and cinnamon. Father Van Den Heuvel and Benetsee had large glasses.

"Du Pré, said Benetsee, "you play fiddle, huh?"

"We got a half hour till we need you to carve," said Madelaine, "so you play the fiddle, I quiet these savages down." She looked at all the small children running, squirming, squealing.

Du Pré got his fiddle, tightened up the bow, tuned. He began to play, nothing in particular, make his fingers fly, they were a little cold. Du Pré played "Baptiste's Lament."

Benetsee pulled a willow flute from his coat, stuck it in the corner of his mouth, Métis way, so your pipe fit in the other.

The fiddle and the willow.

River bottoms, the wagons full of meat, new babies in the bellies of the women. The wind was from the north and smelled of snow. White owls scudded through storms. Coyotes sang, hunted rabbits in teams, the rabbits ran in circles. One lap, fresh coyote.

The old *chansons*.

Du Pré felt for a moment that he was floating through the roof and looking down. An orange county road truck bashed through the snow, little Gabriel laughing in excitement while Catfoot shifted the gears and cursed in Coyote French, some bad English.

Catfoot, he did everything, like a good Métis man.

He even mined for gold, had an ancient little dragline, pull up thirty feet of the old gravels, from the bed of the old Missouri, when it had flowed north to Hudson Bay. The gold was heavy, it sank to bedrock, right there on the bones of the earth, the gold was. Where the river couldn't dig any deeper.

Tens of thousands of years ago, maybe millions, when the Missouri flowed north and east, till the high white glaciers crept down and bulldozed berms to send it to the Gulf of Mexico.

But before that the strong brown waters roiled north. Red River.

❖ C H A P T E R   3 0 ❖

Du Pré came back late, from having taken Madelaine and her kids home. The house was still hot and steaming. The women and Father Van Den Heuvel had washed every dish, wiped every surface. The house still throbbed from all the people.

Maria was running the vacuum over the worn old Sears, Roebuck carpet. She had a kerchief around her head, to soak up the sweat. Du Pré threw open the front and back doors. He turned the thermostat down. The windows had been sealed off for the winter, translucent plastic stapled to the frames.

Maria mopped at her throat with a paper towel. She went to the back door and stood in the cold, hands on her hips and her head back.

"Some fine Thanksgiving," she said, head turned to Du Pré. "Some fine fiddle, some fine Papa."

"Some fine daughter."

They held each other.

"I'm going to be a doctor," said Maria. Du Pré nodded. Last week she was going to business school, start her own company, make something, she hadn't said what.

Du Pré hugged her.

"Benetsee was very sweet," said Maria, "and the Father say a nice grace, remember all the people who are gone, couldn't be here."

Du Pré nodded. He had taken a heaping plate outside, left it on a fencepost for hungry ghosts, any passing by.

The clean cold air felt good. Du Pré looked up, the air from the house was rising out the doors, turning to frosty fog.

"Would it be all right with you I don't have any kids?" said Maria. "I don't think I'll have time, myself."

"You do what you want," said Du Pré. "Jacqueline tell me she just have litters every other year from now on, we're covered."

"Papa!" Laughter.

The house was getting cold. Du Pré shut the doors, turned the furnace back on.

"That old picture album," said Du Pré, "one got Grandpapa's picture in it, you know where it is?"

Maria nodded.

Du Pré had put it away when Catfoot and Maman had been killed. Hurt too much to look at it, Catfoot in his soldier's uniform, Maman in her wedding dress.

Aunty Pauline in her fringed leather dress, standing on a horse that was running very fast. The leather dress was very short. Aunty Pauline had long slender legs, long slender fingers, blond hair, big dark brown eyes, big tits.

Maria shuffled around in the closet a little and brought the book of photographs out. Red leather, black smudges on it, the leather had dried out and cracked a little.

Du Pré opened it. His father's soldier medals were pinned inside the front cover. Nothing big time, Good Conduct Medal, the African Campaign Medal, Italian Campaign Medal. Expert Rifleman's badge. Honorable discharge paper folded and stapled to the cover.

Catfoot's high school graduation picture, breed face, white teeth, on the lawn in his silly gown with his beaming Papa and Mama. Catfoot as soldier boy, hat looked too big on him, he barely made the height for the army.

Catfoot and his bride, Heloise, big smiles, fun night ahead. Catfoot and his bride and the priest, Father Leblanc.

Little Gabriel du Pré, maybe two, fat little knees in short pants. Aunty Pauline behind, big smile, lots of dark lipstick, good-looking woman, holding little Gabriel, squirming.

She used to take me up on her horse, I'd sit between her and the saddlehorn while she made that damn horse fly. Hold on to the horn so hard I don't doubt there are little fingernail marks in the leather. Still got the saddle, maybe I should check.

Aunty Pauline in a white dress, so short it could have been a bathing suit, hair flying, hat on a string dancing behind her, a lariat looping above her, held in one hand, fringed glove on it.

Some fine-looking woman.

Aunty Pauline trick roping. Aunty Pauline in a line of pretty girls, Calgary Stampede, some of those girls no better than they should be, like Aunty Pauline.

Like my mother say that, go tch tch tch.

Aunty Pauline, three husbands, probably a few more by now.

101

"What you lookin' for there, Papa?" asked Maria.

"I think I know something I don't want to," said Du Pré.

Maria shook her head, went off.

Du Pré whistled, few bars from a portage song. Carry them big heavy packs of pelts, maybe carry two.

Soon, he would have to follow his blood north.

Red River.

✤ CHAPTER 31 ✤

B art Fascelli came back, and he called. Please come.

Du Pré drove out to the ranch. There was a big new double-wide trailer next to the well house. A new four-wheel-drive pickup, lot of lights on top of the cab. Dude wagon.

Bart Fascelli had aged ten years, and he trembled sometimes.

"First couple weeks I had bugs crawling underneath my skin," he said. He broke into a cold, greasy sweat, shivered.

"You all right to be out here alone," asked Du Pré. This man was sick, maybe have convulsions or something.

But Bart's eyes were clear and hard, whatever it was he wasn't afraid of it, death, too.

"Hospitals are very boring," said Bart. "I have been a piece of shit all my life. The dogfucker doctors told me I might die, but I don't care. I'm going to work hard, eat good. I can't sleep at night at all. Can't sleep period. I had a favor to ask of you, maybe you pass it around. Please don't come by if you have any booze on you or in you. Thing I want to do most in all the world is get drunk and sleep. I feel like hell. If I drank I'd feel a lot better. I could eat, I could sleep, I could be right back where I was, go through this shit again. I don't want to. I don't know if I can do this. But I'll try."

Du Pré nodded. "What about Booger Tom?" he said. "Old Booger Tom, he drinks some."

"I told him just please stay in his cabin if he's drinking. I am afraid right now to even smell the stuff."

Du Pré sipped his coffee. Bart Fascelli was drinking bottled mineral water. A lot of it. He seemed to be thirsty down to his soul.

Du Pré looked at the corner of the little living room. A prie-dieu, nice one, old, walnut, with a Bible open on it, couple votive candles. Good. Bart, here, calling on all his friends, help me.

Du Pré had seen a couple people die of the booze, livers gone, lot of pain at the end, painkillers didn't work, the liver couldn't send them into the bloodstream or something. Cirrhosis.

Bugs crawling under his skin. Jesus. Du Pré had had the roots of his hair hurt plenty times, sure enough, but nothing close to that.

"You know Father Van Den Heuvel?" said Du Pré.

Bart shook his head.

Of course, the priest for the poor people, he hate this rich bastard, that's what poor Bart think. Now, here, something I can do for him.

"You OK to drive?" said Du Pré.

Bart nodded, looked puzzled.

"What I want you to do, favor to me, is follow me over to the priest's. He's a very clumsy man, can't barely walk, shouldn't swing an ax, maybe hurt himself."

"I can swing an ax," Bart murmured. Du Pré had seen him ride, Bart had grace and power in him for physical things.

"You embarrassed to meet our poor priest. You think that he hate you. Well, I don't know, he got no reason to like you, probably he don't think about it one way or another. But I drop you off there, he's at church this afternoon, hearing confessions, or over at the hospital in Cooper. You split his wood for him, then maybe you talk, eh?"

"Hah," said Bart, "you're a good shrink. The shrink at the hospital told me I didn't ever think of anyone else. I didn't know how. Well, that's not really true, but you know what is?"

Du Pré waited, Bart was searching for the right words.

"I can give people money. I can send someone to help them. But I never have and don't really know how to give anything my own self. To go over to the clumsy priest's and split his wood for him. I can do that, he can help me bind up my soul. But I would never think of doing that, myself. Send money, send someone else. I don't think that I have any value, you know. That I myself with these two hands can do anything but sign a check, make a phone call."

Du Pré nodded, waited. I been sad, but this . . .

"The kind of money I have just poisons," said Bart. "Poisoned us all. Poisoned Gianni, he has been gone now for twenty-five years. Not a trace, not one. Flew to Denver, walked out of the airport, and no one ever heard anything again."

Du Pré nodded. Tell me about it.

"I want to get well. Find out what happened to my brother. My own self. Those teeth you found, they aren't sure. Not enough of them. I want to go back up there, sift

104

that ground you took me to real carefully, see if I can maybe find more, lay poor Gianni to rest, lay me to rest, too."

His own self, thought Du Pré. He could hire specialists, do it right now, but he wants to get well, go up there, sift that earth and find his brother. Hear his brother speak out of the grave. This Bart, he will do all right, if he does it.

I'm pretty sure that I know already, Bart Fascelli, I will in a little while anyway. But I won't say that now.

Fascelli started up his fancy new pickup, followed Du Pré to the priest's. The woodpile was covered in snow. There was a foot of white stacked narrowly on the handle of the ax.

Du Pré got Bart a broom from the little entryway to the Rectory.

When he drove away, Bart was swinging the ax, an easy motion.

All them fencing lessons, thought Du Pré, probably that kung fu crap, too. All that time, tune your body, never play a tune on it worth dick.

Me, I got to go feed my cows.

✦ CHAPTER 32 ✦

Du Pré was shoveling hay into the feedrack. His cows were close around the pickup. He didn't even license the ancient IH truck any more, just used it to do chores on the ranch. The bed of the truck was icy. Du Pré's feet kept slipping when he shifted his weight.

Some of the cows were pulling at the wisps of hay sticking out of the feedrack. The others were bawling. They heaved against the pickup, trying to get at the feed.

When I move this pickup, thought Du Pré, the dummies will know where they are again and go around to the other side where there is plenty of room, but right now they are too confused to know where they are.

Sometimes I feel that stupid. Sometimes I wish I *was* that dumb.

Du Pré saw someone out of the corner of his eye, a man in a tan topcoat wearing cheap hiking boots. The waffle soles so well made to pick up a nice load of cowshit, get it all over your car's rugs.

"Mr. Du Pré?" said the man. "Jotila, FBI. I wondered if I could talk with you for a minute?"

Du Pré looked at him.

"Sure," said Du Pré. "We have coffee. I tell you what, you go to the back door of my house, to the kitchen. I don't got no Dobermans or anything, I got to get this truck out of here so these dumb cows can eat. I will be there in ten minutes."

"I'll just wait," said the FBI man.

So freeze your ass, thought Du Pré. Official business, stand around in the damn cold.

Du Pré forked off the last of the hay, dropped the pitchfork on the hard icy truck bed, struggled over the side and got into the cab. He cranked the old engine, it wheezed to life, he backed it out the open gate. The cows wouldn't stray from the feedrack so long as there was any hay in it.

The FBI man walked behind the truck. When Du Pré looked back the man was straining against the gate, to drop the loop over the post. Well, good, he's ain't hopeless anyway.

Du Pré waited for him to trudge up, led him into the

106

back entryway of the house. Du Pré slipped off his packs. The FBI man struggled with the iced laces on his boots. He got one off, put his foot down in a puddle of icy water. He winced. He took off the other boot. Hit another puddle with that foot.

Du Pré went into the kitchen, the man followed.

"Put them socks on that radiator there," said Du Pré. It already held a couple of pairs, some gloves drying hard like boards.

Du Pré poured coffee. "You like a sandwich or some soup?" he said.

"No," said the agent, "I had a lousy hamburger in Toussaint."

"You still tryin' to find out who shot that fool Sheriff?" said Du Pré.

The agent nodded glumly. Interview everybody over and over, spread a lot of glue, maybe your fly steps in it. Maybe not even the right fly, but we always get our man, even if it's the wrong one. Ask Leonard Peltier.

"You went out there after you were called on the radio," said the agent. He was scribbling in his notebook.

"Yes," said Du Pré, "they been calling me a long time by then."

"Do you know why Fascelli wanted you?"

"Uh, he knew me some, I guess." Drunken asshole Sheriff shows up without a warrant, for Chrissakes, arrest the man, someone outside shoots the Sheriff in the back of the head, the deputies go apeshit and blaze away, you sitting in there with a starter pistol to protect yourself with, you'd want someone you knew, too. Jesus. Shit.

Jotila tapped his gold pencil on the table. Nice pencil, heavy gold, kind you get you want someone to know you own a nice pencil.

"That old cowboy, Booger Tom, he shot the Sheriff, didn't he?" said the agent.

Du Pré's eyebrows shot up.

"I don't know that," said Du Pré. "I didn't get there till it was all over. Long time."

The agent looked wearily at Du Pré. He shut his notebook.

"I have been an agent for fifteen years," he said, "and I have seen the police fuck up a lot, but this is world-class. When those asshole deputies opened up like they were storming a beach or something old Booger Tom must have blown them a kiss, walked away carrying a torch, mooning the dumb fuckers. Not a one of those nitwits looked *behind* them, for Chrissakes."

"They wouldn't," said Du Pré. The deputies, they were scared. They had assault rifles, pump shotguns, bang bang bang.

"Why do you say that they wouldn't?"

"Don't think they had ever been shot at before," said Du Pré. "Besides, when the Sheriff fell over *backwards*, they would have thought that the shot had to come from the house. They don't know much. Head shot, the body falls toward where the shot came from, if that bullet goes through the skull."

"How do you know that?"

"I shoot a lot of deer in the head," said Du Pré. This guy, maybe he wants me to be the killer now. Well, I got six witnesses I was fifteen miles away, so screw him.

"I think I'll ask Booger Tom to take a lie detector test," said the agent.

"He won't do it," said Du Pré. I'll tell him not to, Mr. FBI man. That asshole Sheriff killed his own self, far as I am concerned. You be dumb enough, you be dead. It's the law.

"The Bureau is burning my ass to get something on this case," said the agent Jotila. "I don't want to stay in Butte, Montana, the rest of my life."

Du Pré shrugged. Threaten Booger Tom to me, you prick, I got no use for you at all. I don't know that he did it, mind you, and I do not care to find out if he did.

"Just one of those things," said Du Pré.

The agent nodded glumly.

"I'll go back to beautiful Butte, now," he said.

He pulled on his socks.

✤ CHAPTER 33 ✤

It got to be Christmas. There was some heavy snow, a lot of wind. Du Pré heard the county road trucks going by. Raymond had got a job with them, the pay was good depending on how much it snowed. Du Pré slipped money to Jacqueline anyway, not in front of Raymond, few years he would have a handle on everything. Not that I ever have, Du Pré thought.

Jacqueline had been four months pregnant when she married her Raymond, girl in her position had to be sure that her man didn't shoot no blanks, just bullets, thank you. Lucky Raymond. He loved her, looked at her like a sick calf. He give her babies, she love him back. Get his balls shot off, he have to find a new home.

Du Pré grinned. I got me some strong women, here. The old saying, that the strength of the Métis was the men's humility, but the backbone of the tribe was the women, who gave life itself.

Jacqueline was pregnant again. She was set on having a baby every nine months and one day, as near as Du Pré could figure.

Du Pré heard a truck in his drive, looked out. It was Bart and Father Van Den Heuvel. Since Bart had taken on the task of splitting the priest's wood while the priest had taken on the task of sticking Bart's soul back together they had spent a lot of time together. Bart had his first chance at life and the priest wasn't going to die over some kindling. Lucky folks, Du Pré thought.

Two of them, maybe they ought to get married.

Du Pré opened the door and the two men came in, stamping the snow off as best they could.

Bart was looking much better. His face had lost watery flesh and now there were some lines that the weather had written, lines of age that had been there but stayed smooth because his body was so soaked in booze. Clear eyes, but very tired.

Can't sleep much yet. I've heard about that, worst thing about the booze, you can't even die at night a little, get some rest, stop things from running though your mind. Banging doors.

Du Pré caught himself. He was going to ask the priest if a hot toddy would go down good, cold day.

"Give the father a hot toddy," said Bart, "I'm better now."

The man needs you to do what he says, thought Du Pré. He made two stiff ones, a cup of strong tea for Bart. They sat, sipped, didn't say anything.

"Cards?" said Du Pré, finally, eyes twinkling.

"No," said Bart, "I have a favor to ask."

Bring the priest to back you up, must be a favor too big for the telephone to carry.

I know what it is.

"I have to find out what happened to my brother," said Bart. "I don't know how to go about it, though, and I was talking to Father Van Den Heuvel and he said you were a smart man and knew this place and you could find out if anyone could."

The priest was looking resolutely away. This was between Bart and Gabriel, he was just here for ballast.

"Why me?" said Du Pré. I know fucking well why me, fate, why me.

"You found the skull, which is probably Gianni's. The teeth. You must want to know."

I already know, I think, said Du Pré to himself, under his mustache. But this one, he's right, I have to know for sure.

Du Pré finished his toddy. He got up, made another one, get this cold out of my bones. He poured Bart some more boiling water, there was still lots of good in his teabag. The priest was only half through with his hot whiskey. Du Pré gave him a little more whiskey, hot water, dollop of lemon.

"I am no detective," said Du Pré.

"Please," said Bart. "I can't do it myself, I don't know how. I need to stay here, work my ass off with Booger Tom, pray. Sweat at night, take five showers a day. I'm still nearer dead than alive."

Du Pré looked at the priest. The big man was wiping his glasses so that he wouldn't have to look at anybody.

"What you want me to do?" said Du Pré.

Bart pulled a manila envelope out of the game pouch at the back of his expensive English hunting coat. Good waxed cotton, breathes, thornproof, keeps out the cold winds. Thousand dollars, probably.

"This is what the private detectives my family hired found. It isn't much. My brother flew to Denver. He stayed one night at the Brown Palace. The next morning he bought an emerald necklace. He rented a car. And that was the last that anybody ever saw of him. He must have paid cash for the gas, there were no credit card slips from after the day he picked the car up in Denver. He had a lot of money on him. And a necklace worth seventy-four thousand dollars, 1967 dollars."

"Plenty people kill your brother for that," said Du Pré.

"Whatever," said Bart. His hands started to shake, he trembled. His eyes rolled up in his head, *gaaaacking* sounds came from his throat. He was stiff and shaking.

Father Van Den Heuvel jammed a folded napkin in Bart's mouth. He grabbed Bart in his huge arms and held him till he quit convulsing. He helped him to the living room and laid him out on the couch.

Du Pré stood back, sipping his toddy.

"He'll be all right in a minute," said the priest.

Du Pré nodded. One sick man, this.

"Will you do it?" Father Van Den Heuvel asked, looking at Du Pré. "He'll pay you, give you money for expenses. It might help him."

Bart stirred weakly. His eyes opened.

"Seizure?" he whispered. He shook his head. "Sorry," he said.

"Yes," said the priest. "We don't mind, Bart."

"It's fine," said Du Pré, setting down his glass. "Even if you fuck up, get drunk or something it's fine. You got friends here, Bart, you don't know how to have them but you'll learn."

Bart stared up at the ceiling. His eyes filled with tears.

"I find out who killed your brother," said Du Pré.

Bart slid a black leather envelope out of his coat pocket. He handed it to Du Pré. "There's five thousand in there," he said. "More, any more you might need, call Lawyer Foote at this number." Little card, expensive paper.

"But when I find out," said Du Pré, "you do what I tell you to do about it, you hear? Do what I say."

"Yes," Bart whispered, nodding. "I just want to know."

✤ CHAPTER 34 ✤

Du Pré went to Raymond and Jacqueline's little house for Christmas dinner. Madelaine's people were in town and she didn't want to upset them, someone notice Du Pré knows his way around her house too good, and she an abandoned wife but still married in the eyes of God, and especially her relatives'.

"We all got them aunts," said Du Pré. " 'Cept me, my aunt, she a hooker on a horse, got a lariat, fer Chrissakes.

His third grandchild was so happy to see Grandpère Du Pré he pissed in Grandpère's lap. Thank you, little Dominick.

"I'm sorry," said Jacqueline, mopping Du Pré off. Lots of good that will do, thought Du Pré, sit through dinner now on my soaked nuts. This grandfather shit, well.

"You can wear some of Raymond's underwear, pair of his jeans," said Jacqueline. Raymond had one pair good pants, church pants, he was in them.

Du Pré changed in their bedroom. He rolled his soiled things together, stuck them in the game pouch of his old hunting coat. Benetsee's deer. Blood on the sleeve. He'd forgotten the old man, been too busy. Benetsee, he hadn't come round, either. Hadn't seen him three, four weeks? Thanksgiving? Damn me. I got to go check. Cow asses, where these days go.

"Hey," said Du Pré when he came out, "I better go see about Benetsee. I have forgot him."

"We didn't," said Jacqueline. "Father Van Den Heuvel took him to that Bart's. I would have them here, but . . ."

This tiny house. Even with just Du Pré and Maria extra it was stuffed to bursting. The three little ones slept in a big closet off the tiny bedroom.

When they ate today it would be on a kitchen table made of a full four-by-eight sheet of plywood sitting on the little kitchen table, chairs for four. Raymond had made a bench, too, for the little ones. Plenty of room for the people, plenty of room for the food. Bart, now, he had never had a meal like this one here. Poor bastard.

Raymond carved the turkey. A huge bird, Du Pré had driven all the way to Great Falls for it. Bought stuffing mix, chestnuts, and fresh oysters.

The Métis people had lots of goiter, no iodine. Big throats, till the oysters came. Eat oyster stew one Friday time to time after that. In the old days, the Métis traded for salmon, but the whites they stole the fish, too.

Du Pré wondered who the first Métis to see the ocean was. Most likely they saw Hudson Bay.

Red River.

Tomorrow, Du Pré would drive east and then north, back up the trail of the returning buffalo hunters, the noisy Red River carts. Supposed to be no snow for two days. Hah. This country, it sat out there, breathing, waiting for the winter, like a big white cat and you the mouse.

They ate. Du Pré's grandson added to his legend by throwing up over himself and much of the table. One glob stuck to the side of Du Pré's wineglass. Du Pré stuck out a finger, wiped it off, looked at the lump, smeared it on his napkin.

"Oh, poor baby," said Jacqueline, grabbing the boy.

"Good, strong Métis stomach," said Du Pré. "He throw it far, that little one."

"Papa!" said Jacqueline, laughing. She took her baby to the sink, put him in it, washed him while shushing his wails.

"So you go see Aunty Pauline," said Jacqueline, returning. Little Dominick, damp and streaked, much subdued. The boy pecked at a fresh plate of food, eyeing distances, computing trajectories.

"Yes," said Du Pré, "I haven't seen her in a long time. Got some time, travel a little." He'd given Jacqueline a thousand dollars, to keep against need. Hard-headed girl. Raymond wouldn't even know until they were up against it. Just keep them shots coming, Raymond. Got to make them babies, regular-like.

Raymond looked around the table with pride. Jacqueline loved him enough to let him keep that.

Jacqueline had made a wild plum pie. Gathered the fruit from the bushes that hugged the little creek that ran behind the house. Baby in the little carrier on her back. Rum in the pie. Nutmeg.

I should have brought my fiddle with me, thought Du Pré. Well, I am going to take it with me, see those fiddlers up there know what they are about. Yes.

Du Pré poured whiskey in his coffee. Raymond had a little. The boy hardly drank. Boy, hell, man, got more kids than I do. I was that young once, but I drank lots more whiskey.

Maria sat very quietly, in her sister's house. Jacqueline had the babies, had proved herself. Du Pré looked at Maria,

115

felt a little sorry for the world, it didn't lie down, do like she said. He laughed, shook his head. My girls.

Tomorrow I go back up that trail, drive first to Pembina, over in North Dakota, then right up past the little Catholic churches every twenty miles on the prairie. Once the Church had railroad cars made up like chapels for weddings, baptisms, funerals. Park it on a siding of the Canadian Pacific, tend to business.

That night Du Pré slept badly, excited, things gnawing at his mind. He dreamed, bad confusing dreams.

He woke up choking, in this house he had been born and raised in.

He remembered being in the little bedroom, the one that Maria had now, one night a very long time ago.

His parents had been talking low, in bed.

His mother, she had been crying.

♣ CHAPTER 35 ♣

Just one more piece Métis trash headed north, Du Pré thought. Them English hate us Frenchies, hate the Indians, see what it is like to come from an island. Carry it with you in your soul.

North Dakota in winter. Bleak. Du Pré recalled the joke, the big North Dakota winter sport, get the neighbors to help push the house down the road, jump-start the furnace.

He stopped at a gas station for coffee.

Aunty Pauline was in the little Manitoba town of Boissevain, not so far over the border. Du Pré had called her. She had a wonderful voice, the voice you get from many years of cigarettes and whiskey and broken loves.

Du Pré couldn't remember if she sang or not. He hoped so.

He wondered what she looked like now, sixty-some, he remembered her blond and beautiful and very strong. How his mother looked at her, not liking her. Too wild. Bring that out in Catfoot, she'd have trouble, threaten my house, my little Gabriel, I don't like her.

Dangerous women, they scare women not so dangerous.

The border. The Canadian side, man leaned down, asked where Du Pré is going, how long he plans to stay. Du Pré said a week maybe. Then they toss the car, even took out the seats while Du Pré sat in the waiting room, looking at a bronze plaque which stated the stiff penalties for beating the shit out of a customs officer.

It took Du Pré two hours to put his car back together. They had left his fiddle case open on the hood in the bitter cold. The fiddle's varnish had begun to wrinkle.

Take that, you Frenchy Indian piece of shit, we don't care you call yourself American.

The Scots were the worst. Live in the mountains on an island, invent haggis, you'd have a sour view of the world, too.

Fuck you, Du Pré thought.

Gabriel Dumont. If poor mad Louis Riel had let him, little Gabriel would have killed your precious General Wolseley, your redcoat troops, left you dead there. Spit in your faces.

Du Pré spat on the asphalt, all rimed with salt. So many people from the cities, never saw ice on the road. Come booming up here from Chicago, wherever, car set on cruise control, hit a patch of ice and that's that.

But he liked the country. It felt like home. Very big sky, this. The Scandinavians broke under it, often enough. The North Dakota State Motto: I bain don't tink dis luek like Norvay . . .

Manitoba. Good woodland Cree word, or was it Chippewa? No English word good enough to name this country, for sure. Red River, I piss here it goes to Hudson Bay.

The road went north, straight as a stretched string. Long, lone, and a little up, long, lone, and a little down.

Boissevain. Little Catholic town, Métis town, little white church, very big graveyard.

Du Pré went to the saloon. Remembered that in Canada, the bars were divided, men single in one end, couples in another. The Canadians, they didn't like fights.

Du Pré called his Aunty Pauline. Man answered, seemed about to hang up, but he called her to the phone instead.

"I'll come there," she said, voice deep and smoky. "I look a lot different. Do you?"

Du Pré said yes.

He had a Molson beer, squat bottle with scratches on it. All Canadian beer bottles were the same, so they could take them back to any brewery.

Du Pré rolled a cigarette, smoked, thought his aunt would be a little while, put on a face, must take longer these days, try to sketch in what had fallen off.

But she came right away. Wearing crimson buckskins, cigarette in a long holder. She smiled at the barman, who smiled back.

My Aunty Pauline, the character. Du Pré liked her.

She was still a good-looking woman. Silk shirt, soft around the throat. Hard face, thick coat of makeup. Brown eyes very big still, lots of green eye shadow.

"So, Du Pré," she said, sitting down. Cheap large stones on her hands, or maybe even expensive ones. Du Pré couldn't tell. The shoulders of her crimson leather jacket were damp from the wet snow falling outside.

They didn't hug, didn't kiss. Aunty Pauline looked down, the barman brought her a drink brown over ice. Brandy? Du Pré paid for it, left the change.

"What you want?" she said. "All these years you don't want to talk to your Aunty Pauline, now you do. Your mother never like me."

"I got a question," said Du Pré. "Then I'll leave you alone."

Pauline sipped her brandy.

"You have a lover once, man named Fascelli? Gianni Fascelli?"

Du Pré waited a moment.

"Aunty Pauline," said Du Pré, "you hear me?"

She had frozen. Drink in hand. Her hand shook. She set her drink down.

"No," she said finally.

"I think that I know better," said Du Pré, "you know?"

"Look," said Aunty Pauline. "This Fascelli man, he sees me ride in a show, OK? He fall in love with me, crazy love. He has lots of money, sends me gifts, follows me around the circuit. Miles City, he's in the stands, Havre, Calgary, Spokane, all around. But he scares me. He has crazy eyes, he's always drunk, he has so much damn money."

Du Pré nodded, sipped his beer.

"So I tell him to leave me alone."

Du Pré had another swallow.

"He gets mad with me one night, threatens me with all these gangster people in Chicago he knows. I don't go with him, he have me killed. So I meet him at a hotel, stay in his bed three days. I'm very scared."

Du Pré nodded.

"He pass out drunk, I get up, dress, grab my suitcase, run to Catfoot, hide."

"So he was looking for you?" And, thought Du Pré, the money in his wallet and left nut, most likely.

"He sent people to ask questions, sent gifts, too, said he would be by soon, and just take me with him."

Du Pré looked at her. We don't none of us got a straight story, he thought, but poor Aunty Pauline.

"So that's what you know now," she said. "I got a younger man now, he's very jealous, so I got to go."

Du Pré nodded.

He watched his aunt walk away. Still had a nice ass, must be she still ride some. Whatever.

♣ CHAPTER 36 ♣

Du Pré fiddled. He stood in his Métis finery out in front of the bandstand, lights on him, while the people clapped and danced and cheered. People mostly looked a lot like him, some few English.

The men wore a lot of white with red sashes, the women silks in brilliant colors, white teeth in brown faces.

A man bowed from a life on horseback, hands twice the size they should be for his height, he played the good ringing bones. Somebody had a washtub bass, they pulled on the string and broomstick and the bottom bowed up, slide that deep note.

Good people.

120

Du Pré fiddled till his fingers hurt, found himself scooting off from the playing of the others, dropping little clusters of icy notes back down on the melody.

He was knee-walking, grass-grabbing drunk. Couldn't lie on the floor without holding on.

Some people took him home with them, saying these Manitoba Provincial Police bad on drunk drivers, love to arrest people from the States.

Du Pré awoke the next morning, still pretty drunk. He was asleep in a cupboard bed, under a bunch of quilts. He sat up, and he smiled, thought about the night before.

The master of ceremonies had unfurled what he said was the new Canadian flag. A big green frog pissing on nine little beavers. Du Pré began laughing again, thinking about that flag.

Smell of smoked venison frying, slap of spoon mixing up the pancake batter.

Du Pré sat down at a long trestle table. He looked up, looked down, seemed like he was looking at a bunch of cousins.

"You got the big head, he?" said one man, about Du Pré's age. When he smiled, he had no upper front teeth. Oh. That man, one of the fiddlers from the night before.

"Oh," said a plump pretty woman, "you play that fiddle good." She set down a platter of venison, big platter of fry bread.

Peppersauce for the venison, chokecherry jam for the fry bread.

I feel like home here, thought Du Pré. Montana, it is home, I know, I like it, I will die there, but my people are up here too.

Du Pré was famished. He ate and ate till the hosts clapped and laughed at him.

"He need a good woman feed him more," said a man

at the other end of the table. "They got no good women down in them States, eh? You take one of ours back, eh?"

Du Pré blushed, he thought of Madelaine.

Now I got to go all the way over to Moose Jaw, the Oblate Fathers Home, see that old Father Leblanc.

He can't break the secrets of the confessional, but I have to know this.

I have to know all of this.

After the big breakfast, one of the men drove Du Pré back to his old cruiser. Du Pré felt a little dirty, he'd sweated a lot in the stage lights. He was still wearing all the fine clothes that his women had made for him, leggings, sash, silk shirt, kerchief, vest, hat, moccasins. He had a flight feather from a red hawk in his hat band now, someone had given it to him the night before.

Métis man with a hangover, fiddle on the seat beside him, smell of rum and cheap tobacco, going down the road in a old car with American license plates.

No one stopped him. He drove through the little towns, some English, some Métis, the old Red River country, must have been some fine country once, before the English.

This air, I know it, Du Pré thought, breathing deep. It was cold out, but he drove with the window down, to clear his head.

He stopped for lunch in a little Catholic town, asked the man at the garage where there was a good cheap little motel. The man at the motel looked like Du Pré and charged him fifteen dollars for the night.

He bathed and changed into jeans and boots and a sheepskin vest, waxed cotton coat, put on his battered Stetson. Packed the Métis finery away, he would take it out the next time he found a fiddling contest, here or back over the border.

Du Pré was in no real hurry.

The next morning he went to confession, went to Mass. He asked the priest where he could buy a pretty missal. He paid the priest a hundred dollars for one, a beautiful thing, cover by some Métis woman, soft white deerskin, beaded, quilled, the priest said it was a hundred years old. Some of the pages were stained, it looked like the marks of tears.

This book had lived some, that's for sure.

He found a quick dry-clean place, had his scarf and sash and shirt cleaned. Now I am ready for the next fiddling, yes.

Moose Jaw. It couldn't be any place else, this place that did need to be named Moose Jaw. He didn't care why it was named that.

The Oblate Fathers Home was a big old brick building, well kept, a lot of pretty junipers around it, the white trunks of birches. Chapel right off the entrance. Du Pré went in, crossed himself, and he prayed for a while.

He asked where Father Leblanc was. The attendant led him down a brightly polished hallway, floors and walls of maple and birch. He motioned Du Pré into a room, a small one with leaded windows and bright chintz curtains. A narrow bed, a desk, a prie-dieu. Father Leblanc was slumped, boneless, in a heavy old leather chair.

His old head and face were hairless, so wrinkled he looked like a ball of string. He wheezed and whistled, dreaming.

"I won't bother him now," said Du Pré. "I am one of his old flock. I will wait here till he wakes."

Du Pré took out the missal, opened it to the page marked by the faded blue silk ribbon, read.

Father Leblanc slept.

✤ CHAPTER 37 ✤

Du Pré's Latin wasn't so good, never had been.

He closed the missal, looked out the window at what was left of the day. Not too far back, it was the shortest day of the year. He was some farther north here, the shadows seemed longer, the blue in them colder.

Winters used to be much tougher, back in the time of the grandfathers. And there had not been so much to fight the winter with.

Or hunger.

Or cold.

Father Leblanc stirred. His sagging old eyelids lifted, he looked for a moment like a very old turtle.

Father Leblanc blessed Du Pré.

"You don't remember me," said Gabriel, pulling off his hat. He leaned close, put his face near to the old man's. "Can you hear me, Father Leblanc?"

"Yes," the old priest said, his voice a wet whisper, "I think I know you. Are you not the son of Guillaume du Pré?"

"That was my father, Catfoot," said Gabriel. "You know, you baptized me, gave me my first communion."

The old priest's eyes moved slowly to the gathering dark out his window. He pushed a little button on a cord pinned to the sleeve of his cassock.

The attendant came in a few minutes. Father Leblanc ordered some tea.

The old priest asked questions of the Toussaint people, who had married, who had babies, how was the youngster Van Den Heuvel?

Du Pré answered. They sipped tea.

"But I didn't come here for a simple visit," said Gabriel, "I have a question for you. So I must tell you what I know. Then I will ask you the question, and when I do, I will offer you the missal here . . ."

He let the old priest look at it. His eyes were infinitely sad. Du Pré took it back.

"My father, Catfoot, he killed a man named Gianni Fascelli, cut off his head and his hands and put them up in the mountains, next to an old plane wreck had a couple other skeletons. This man, this Fascelli, was an animal, my father killed him because he loved his sister, my aunt Pauline, and this man was threatening her. Us Métis, you don't mess with our women."

The old priest was still, looking out the window.

"So I know all that," said Du Pré, "figured out some more things, too, but they are not very important. But I need to know this, for my father's soul, and I don't want you to say anything. I need you to sin just a little for me, Father Leblanc."

Du Pré picked up the old man's hand, wrapped it around the missal.

"What I need to know is did my father feel bad about killing this man. Did Catfoot repent and ask God's mercy? That's all. I need to know that. So if he did, I want you to take this missal, and if he didn't, I want you to let it go. For the living, I want you to sin just a little."

The old priest looked at Gabriel with his sad patient eyes.

The old hand clamped shut on the missal. The old priest pulled the little book away.

Du Pré bowed his head and wept. The old priest reached

out, made the sign of the cross on Du Pré's forehead with his thumb, fingers light as smoke on Du Pré's skin.

Du Pré looked up, nodded.

"I thank you for the living, Father," said Du Pré.

The old man was looking out at the dark. He held the missal lightly in his hands, his lips moved.

Du Pré picked up his hat and left. Outside the cold winter air stung the tears on his cheeks.

He drove down into Moose Jaw, found a motel, put the fiddle in his room so it wouldn't get frozen. There were some restaurants close by, Du Pré ate a bad supper of overcooked beef and vegetables that had been simmered so long they were transparent mush.

He walked on, found a saloon, went in and had some whiskeys.

He went back to his motel, there was a stupid movie on the television, fine with Du Pré.

Well, Du Pré thought, I know it all but for that last thing with the priest before I come up here. But it was the only question that was important, can't bring the life back to any of them, can't pull the bullet out of time, can't do much. But Papa, he have hot blood and a lot of pride, and I am glad he apologized to God for his sin, there, that his pride didn't take and carry him all the way up to that damn train. Well, Catfoot, now I go and clean up the last of it. You old bastard.

He went to sleep and slept till midmorning, with his fiddle asleep on the table beside him.

Du Pré drove south the next day, down toward Montana, down the route that Gabriel Dumont had taken, thousands of English hunting him. The little man slipped through them all, drifted through the Cypress Hills, down to Montana forever.

Spent the rest of his days not talking to priests.

126

✦ CHAPTER 38 ✦

D u Pré," said Madelaine, when he stood in her doorway, tired from the road. "Du Pré, I think that you find everything that you were looking for, eh?" She kissed him.

Du Pré nodded. Well, not exactly, but he knew pretty much where everything was, pretty soon he'd have everything, everyone paid, the loose ends all knotted off. Then what? More grandkids, piss in my lap.

"You hungry, Du Pré?" Madelaine pushed a strand of dark hair back from her forehead. Little gray in it, looked very good. She was not a vain woman, dye her hair, look foolish. Du Pré smiled, loving her.

"Yes," said Du Pré, grabbing her, lifting her up, carrying her to the bedroom.

"Du Pré!"

After, they lay laughing for a while. Madelaine ran her finger over Du Pré's chest, nuzzled his ear.

"I miss you. You find your crazy aunt?"

"Yes," said Gabriel. "You know, I love my aunt, but I don't think she will have it. She got a young, jealous man, don't sound good."

"You got an old jealous woman here. You play your fiddle for them Red River women, eh? You forget your Madelaine?"

"Just the six times," said Du Pré, "I'm so drunk, maybe more."

Madelaine whacked him, not hard.

"You not like that," she said, propping herself up on her elbow. "Too good a man, hurt those who love you. Six, maybe more, some bullshit, Du Pré. Hah."

Du Pré looked at the ceiling. She got me there.

"That Bart working horses with Booger Tom, he get kicked, got his leg in a cast now," said Madelaine. "I don't think nothing else happened while you were gone. Maria comes by every day, we are going to be all right, now she got something to look after besides you."

"What?" said Du Pré, "she got a new boyfriend?"

"Oh, no," said Madelaine. "She got no time for a boyfriend. Now she is studying to be a senator, she says."

"Oh," said Du Pré. She go to Helena one time, but Washington? Never. Oh, God. Senator Du Pré, the one in the miniskirt. Don't you got to be old, like twenty-five or something?

"So what you find up there," said Madelaine.

Du Pré didn't say anything.

"Don't tell me, huh?"

"I don't tell anybody till I have it all right here, in my hand," said Du Pré. He closed his fist, gripped hard.

Madelaine grumbled about it a little.

"You see Benetsee?" said Du Pré.

Madelaine shook her head. The old man hadn't been in church this last Sunday, but then he often didn't come to church. But the smoke was coming up from his chimney, so he had to be all right.

They got dressed. Du Pré yawned, he was all off in his sleep, been making too much road, found out too much, he was worried about his aunt.

Write her? Say when your young man leave you you remember your nephew down here? She would hate him forever for his pity. What Pauline would do, get dead drunk, drive her car very fast, point it into something big. *Waaahaaaaaaaaaaaaaaaaa. Bam.*

She was plenty tough, all right. Tough herself to death, that girl.

I am glad that Maria doesn't much like horses, thought Du Pré, she's the same tough, but at least she have a chance. Pauline, there is just a poor girl with big tits and good legs.

"Well," said Du Pré, "I got to go now, see that Bart and the old man."

Madelaine nodded.

Du Pré's car smelled a little of garbage. He had a paper sack full of browning apple cores and sandwich wrappings. He drove to the Toussaint Bar, put the sack in the trash bin at the side of the place, along with the empty bottles and the soggy napkins and paper plates from their lousy hamburgers.

The Toussaint Bar, where love is suddenly taken drunk.

Pauline, you ought to come down here, not stay up there alone, down here you got family.

Old Benetsee, now he's family, too. Spooky old man, lived on nothing, people brought him food, fixed his window it got broken. Split his wood. Benetsee, wheezy old dogs, wheezy old man with his flute in the side of his mouth.

Thing is, thought Du Pré, since we invent writing we remember too much and forget the important things.

Du Pré drove away. The day was warm and overcast and there was a black smudgy line on the northern horizon, soon they would have an Alberta Clipper run down the front of the Rockies, make the windows rattle in their frames.

Glad I come down before that thing, thought Du Pré. Most storms came from the west, the ones from the north

129

were in a bigger hurry and they dumped a lot more snow.

Du Pré knocked on Benetsee's door. He heard a chair slip on dirty linoleum, the old man pushed back the faded calico curtain and peered out at Du Pré. He smiled, couple teeth here and there. Very yellow, brown at the roots.

"Du Pré!" said Benetsee, "good to see you! Some wine, you bring?"

Du Pré shook his head.

"You go get some then, or I don't talk to you," said Benetsee. He shut the door, real firm.

Du Pré did as he was told.

♣ C H A P T E R   3 9 ♣

Benetsee, playing the flute, glass of cheap white on the table, stuck there among the crumpled papers and bread rinds, a cut of venison black and dried, some apples as wrinkled as the old man.

Benetsee, playing his flute, looping melodies, came from somewhere Du Pré had never been. Played until Du Pré fidgeted, then he stopped the tune. Chop.

"So," said Benetsee, "you find out some things, maybe too much?"

Du Pré nodded. He wasn't going to tell anyone anything until he had dug up the rest. Not Madelaine, not Maria, not Bart, and for sure not this old fart.

"That Red River country pretty good, huh?"

Du Pré nodded.

More flute. Was there a point to all this?

The old man stopped again. He got up, shuffled over to a shelf, took down his bundle of deerskin, brought it to the table. He undid the thongs, unrolled it.

Pipe bowls. Just some hunks of rock, some the rude shape hacked out, others smoothed down perfectly, ready for a willow stem. The red stone glowed, seemed to have some light within.

Benetsee poked around in the pipe bowls, picked up one, set it back down, picked up another.

"This one," he said. He belched, held out his glass. Du Pré unscrewed the cap of the jug, poured him more wine.

"This stuff kill you, you know," said Du Pré.

"I just die sometime," said Benetsee. "Nothing kill me. I just die when I want to."

OK. OK.

Benetsee reached down by the table, brought up a quiver, one full of willow pipe stems. He selected one, white as paper, pared the butt with his pocketknife, twisted and jammed it into the smokehole. Dug a little pipestone mouthpiece out of the rubble in the bundle. Carefully pulled off some strands of sinew from a smelly little bunch on the table. He lashed the sinew three places on the pipestem. Took a little leather pouch from his stained old coat, fished out a wad of feathers.

Red-shafted flicker. Bright crimson quills, soft black and gray barbules. He fixed the feathers to the sinew lashings, two, three, two.

"Here," said Benetsee, offering the pipe to Du Pré.

Du Pré took it, looked at it close, held it away from his eyes. Carving of a bobcat, back arched, paws on a grouse, grouse with feathered leggings, so it was winter. Not a bobcat, tufts on the ears, so it was a lynx.

"Pretty soon you smoke that," said Benetsee. "You know when and where and for which man. Smoke it,

131

watch the smoke rise, go to his tired soul on the Star Trail.''

Du Pré rolled a cigarette, handed it to Benetsee, made himself another.

They smoked. The old man had pinched a little tobacco from the end of his cigarette, rubbed it in his fingers, dribbled the tiny flakes on the pipe bowls in the deerskin bundle.

Du Pré left, he drove away from the old man's with the pipe beside him on the seat.

Bart's truck was parked by his trailer, the curtains on the window were open. When Du Pré knocked he saw Bart through the window in the door. Bart struggled up from the couch and stumped on over.

He looked out at Du Pré and smiled.

Du Pré looked down. I got news, can't tell you yet, one last thing here before I do. So fire me.

''Du Pré!'' said Bart. Each time Du Pré saw Bart's face he looked older but better, his face was running hard to catch up to time, even over sharp rocks.

Du Pré looked down at the walking cast, up to the knee, a rubber heelpiece.

''Booger Tom said I was only thirty breaks away from being some kind of horseman,'' said Bart, real proud, beaming. I got hurt and I didn't get drunk, I am winning big.

Du Pré came in. Bart hobbled to the little kitchen, made tea.

They sipped the tea, didn't speak for a while.

''Well?'' said Bart finally.

''I got most of it,'' said Du Pré. ''Just one or two more things, I think, then I will have the whole story.'' I got the whole damn story, I just need . . . the things that aren't just words.

''OK,'' said Bart.

"But I'm going to wait to tell you until I have those last one, two pieces, you don't mind." Even if you do mind.

Bart shook his head, smiled. Fine. You do what you have to.

"Here," said Du Pré, "is the rest of your money. It didn't cost that much." He pulled out a stained envelope, dropped it on the coffee table.

"Keep it," said Bart. "Give it to Van Den Heuvel if you don't want it. No, you keep it, you should be paid for your time. I insist."

Du Pré nodded. He took the money back. For the oatmeal for my grandchildren, soon we buy it by truckload.

"You want to help me find these last one, two pieces, eh?" said Du Pré.

"Of course," said Bart. "Is a pig's prick pork?"

Du Pré snorted. "We got to wait until there is some warm weather, spring most likely, then we will need a big diesel shovel."

Bart nodded.

"Just the two of us," said Du Pré. "We look for these things."

"I can order up any piece of equipment we need any time," said Bart.

Du Pré looked down at Fascelli's cast.

"That hurt a lot?"

"Some," said Bart, "but not too bad. I try to ignore it. Booger Tom would have ignored the broken leg altogether."

"Well," said Du Pré, "what I will need is a guy who knows how to run one of those big diesel shovels, see, we got to move a lot of gravel, thousands of tons, move it real carefully. So I need a real good guy, stir his coffee with the bucket on that shovel."

"I'll hire the best," said Bart.

"No," said Du Pré. "Just you and me, huh?"

"Oh," said Bart, "I become that real good guy with that shovel, stirring his coffee with the bucket?"

Du Pré nodded. I'll be down by that damn bucket, he thought, you better be good.

"I'll take care of it," said Bart.

Du Pré nodded.

"My own self," said Bart.

Du Pré nodded.

❖ CHAPTER 40 ❖

Bitter cold day, wind so cold that it burned.

Du Pré stood by the chute, looking hard through his frosted lashes at the steers' hides, the brands, some of them messed over with frozen shit. Messed over too damn artfully.

Days like this, I should have been a brain surgeon, thought Du Pré, indoor work anyway.

He reached out, rubbed hard on the green smears on a steer's rump. That one, that one is worked over, god damn it. This guy, I have been thinking of him like that for some time now.

Du Pré stepped down from the chute, his boots sliding on the welded pipe the thing was built of.

The rancher was huddled down against the cold.

"Mr. Higgins," said Du Pré, hard against the wind, "those brands are reworked. No way I sign off on this one. Your cattle here are impounded till we know who they belong to."

The man straightened right up.

"Bullshit," he screamed. He had two sons with him, they heard the noise, didn't know what it meant yet, but they started to walk over to Du Pré and their father.

Du Pré ran to his car, got in, started the engine, flicked on the radio. "Du Pré here," he said quickly. "Say, I got a bunch of bad brands, the Higgins place, you get someone out here, do it now."

"Got it," said the dispatcher.

Higgins smashed Du Pré's window with a crowbar. His sons were behind him. Everyone yelling but Du Pré.

Du Pré scrabbled in the glove box for his gun. Higgins had bashed the glass mostly in. Du Pré grabbed his .38, opened the far door, slid out and stood.

Higgins came at him around the car, screaming, crowbar in his hand.

Du Pré aimed low and shot him in the leg, aiming for the kneecap.

The man folded up. The sons were unbuttoning their coats.

"Shit shit shit shit," said Du Pré to himself, running toward the stock tank, good heavy-gauge metal, I hope.

He glanced back. Both sons were down on the ground with their father, one had a gun in his hand.

"You drop that!" Du Pré yelled. The son looked up, started to lift the pistol. Du Pré fired. The son slammed into the side of Du Pré's old cruiser.

Shit shit shit shit.

The second son looked over at Du Pré, terrified. Sirens down the road, coming on quick.

"Don't shoot! Don't shoot!"

He raised his hands. Higgins was on the ground, writhing, his leg clamped in his hands. The other son was against Du Pré's tire, and looking too damn still.

Sirens. Come on come ON.

The Sherrif's car was just a quarter-mile away and closing real fast. Du Pré thought the dispatcher might have heard the glass break when Higgins started in with the crowbar. Whatever.

Wonder if that guy knew what he was doing, when he lifted up that gun. I don't know. What else could I do but shoot? Not shoot. Shit.

Du Pré wished that he hadn't fired, probably would wish that for the rest of his life. Nothing clean about this at all.

The Sheriff's car came into the turnaround and slid sideways on the frozen mud. Deputy came out of the car with a pump shotgun in his hands, pointing it at Du Pré.

"No!" Du Pré screamed, standing up and dropping his gun. "Them! God damn it! Them!" He pointed over at the three by his car.

Higgins was flat on his back now, his forearms pointing straight up. The son that Du Pré had shot looked very dead. Bundle of dirty clothes. The other boy was on his knees, hands raised very high, screaming don't shoot don't shoot don't shoot.

Oh, God, thought Du Pré, how does all this happen over a little bad money? Things gone to hell, just like that.

The deputy was too lightly dressed for the wind. He walked forward, waving the shotgun. The son on his knees went flat on his face. The deputy went to him, handcuffed his wrists behind his back.

Higgins had passed out from the pain.

Du Pré knelt by the man that he had shot. He reached out his hand, pressed a thumb against the man's throat. Nothing.

Some fine day this. Du Pré's groin burned with cold. Pissed his pants.

136

"Du Pré," said the deputy, "you're bleeding, man."

Du Pré looked at his belly. Little blood running down his left pant leg. Big black scorch mark on his coat.

"God damn!" said Du Pré. "I am one fine law enforcement officer! I shot myself, I think!" I get a combat brand inspector's badge, sure enough. Ain't this some shit.

He looked up. It was quiet. High above, an eagle soared.

✦ C H A P T E R   4 1 ✦

D u Pré sat on the examining table, looking incuriously at the furrow he had plowed in his belly, calculating an inch that way, two inches that way, hoo boy.

The doctor bent over, scrubbed at the wound. Du Pré winced, but didn't feel anything except the scrubbing noise through his flesh. *Scritch scritch scritch.*

"You're lucky," said the doctor. "Just a superficial skin tear. All stippled with powder, though, some of it will fester. The scar will look like some kid was stabbing you with a pencil."

Higgins had been flown out to Miles City, his knee was shattered. The son Du Pré had shot was dead, shot right through the heart.

" 'Scuse me," said Du Pré. He lurched over to the wastebasket and threw up. The doctor waited.

When Du Pré quit heaving he went back and sat on the table again.

The doctor finished sewing him up, put a bandage on the wound, gave him a shot.

"Just lie down for a while," said the doctor, going out the door.

The acting Sheriff Benny Klein came in.

"How you feel?" he said.

"Shit how I feel. I just kill somebody, shoot myself over some damn hamburger meat. I feel like shit, that's what."

Benny had a clipboard, a little tape recorder.

"Guy bashed in the window, I am scrambling out the other side, must have shot myself then, I run to the stock tank, shoot back . . . no, I shot Higgins in the leg, then I run to the stock tank, shoot back, guy falls over, other one sticks up his hands . . ."

How long all this death and pain take, ten seconds? Fifteen?

Du Pré did not mention how the deputy pointed the gun at him first. All in all, it was not a day to remember well.

"Yeah," said Benny, "things are always confused. Only time I was ever shot at was up at Fascellis, we all panicked and fired everything every which way like we was at Dien Bien Phu or something. And no one even fired at my ass, except the Sheriff was dead on his back on the lawn. You know how many times the four of us fired? Eighty-one. I never heard a one of them."

Du Pré felt weak and sick.

"OK," said the Sheriff, "I got to suspend you pending the investigation. Got to have you turn in your gun."

Du Pré didn't offhand know where his gun was. Pocket of my coat, maybe. And it is hanging right over there. Du Pré got up, went to it, fished around, brought out the old pistol. Cocked. Safety off, live rounds in it. Oh, god damn it all to three kinds of hell.

Du Pré let the hammer down, spun the cylinder, two rounds gone, three left.

"See," said Du Pré pointing, "here, this first one is

where I shot myself because I was behaving in a threatening manner, the second is where I killed Higgins's kid because *he* was behaving in a threatening manner."

"Hey, calm down," said Benny. "You seem to be in shock or something. We can do this later, you know, but I have to take the gun." He tugged the gun out of Du Pré's hand and dropped it into an evidence bag.

"You rest up, you hear?" said Benny.

"I'm sorry," said Du Pré.

There was someone screaming down the hall, probably Higgins's wife.

"Get drunk," said Benny. "Get drunk, rest up, back on the horse."

Us cowboys, thought Du Pré, we sure keep it simple, yes. He nodded, began pulling on his clothes.

A nurse stuck her head in the door. "We'd like you to stay tonight," she said. "You might be in shock."

"I just killed a man," said Du Pré, "and I am in shock, yes, but I will not stay here tonight."

"So," she said. "Well, you take care and we're here if you need us."

"Du Pré," said Madelaine from the doorway. Maria was looking in over her shoulder.

They had both been crying.

"Tell you two what," said Du Pré. "You are lookin' for a hero, I am not him. Me, I want to go home, start on the south end of a half-gallon of whiskey, go all the way to the North Pole."

Madelaine and Maria looked at him. They grinned. "Sure," they chorused. "Maybe we go along with you," said Maria.

Du Pré signed himself out of the hospital, against medical advice. Goddamned right. Lots of people, they die around these quacks. Happens all the time.

That other time, that guy was just reaching for a rifle, I shot him but he lived. Got a suspended sentence. This Higgins boy, he is dead. That old man Higgins, I hope that he gets gangrene in that knee, goes all the way up to his scalp. After it gets his balls.

Du Pré sat in Maria's car, between her and Madelaine.

"How come you got this car, you aren't old enough to get a driver's license yet without I sign for it, and I ain't signed for nothing," said Du Pré. "You just lucky I am one suspended law enforcement officer."

"Shut up, Papa," said Maria. She drove off. When she came to the stop sign at the parking lot entry to the street she put out an arm to keep Du Pré from slamming into the dash at half a mile an hour.

"OK," said Du Pré, "I let you take care of me, don't talk back."

"What you want to eat?" said Madelaine.

Du Pré said he didn't want to eat for a while, maybe a couple of years.

They dropped Madelaine at her house, her kids would be wondering where she was.

"I see you in a little while," she said, kissing Du Pré.

"Go to the bar," said Du Pré to Maria. "I get some whiskey."

He bought three bottles, opened one of them on the drive to his house, drank a big slug and felt very dizzy.

Du Pré barely made it into the house. He staggered to the bed and fell on it and slept.

✤ CHAPTER 42 ✤

"We some fine pair, eh?" said Du Pré, looking at Bart's cast. Du Pré was walking comma-shaped, so as not to stretch his stitched stomach.

Bart had stuck his hand in something mean. It was bandaged, and he moved it very, very gingerly.

The chinook wind had come, warm from the north and west, most of the snow had melted off, there were pools of water on the frozen ground. Du Pré's soaked cows were pulling hay out of the feedrack, grimly chewing. No place to lie down, chew their cud. Soon it would get very cold again, and the world would be glazed hard and very difficult to stand on.

"Where do we need this big shovel, anyway," said Bart.

Du Pré rolled a cigarette. He lit it.

"Oh," he said, " 'bout ten or twelve miles from here, old mining claim of my father's."

"Your father had a mine?" said Bart. That, too.

"Gold claim," said Du Pré. Probably an emerald necklace down there, few other things, like an old car. Under the gravels, in the old riverbed. The Red River.

Go all the way down to bedrock, then there is no more story. Just the old earth, keeping the rest of its secrets.

"You go to big diesel shovel school?" said Du Pré. He looked at Bart's cast hard.

"Correspondence course," said Bart. "Lotsa pictures."

Mail-order course. Shit shit shit.

141

"Yeah," said Bart, "I was reading this stupid magazine, found an ad, said make big money, learn to operate heavy equipment. So I sent off for the stuff."

"Oh," said Du Pré, looking at his cigarette.

"When I was a kid, I had a couple toys, one of them was a big diesel shovel. I loved it the most. I have a deep and heartfelt, spiritual understanding of big diesel shovels. Trust me."

"OK," said Du Pré. He started to laugh. Bart, here, he is learning a lot from old Booger Tom. Laugh at snakebite, broken bones and let's do something even if it's wrong. Horse throw you, get back on till one of you is dead or you are moving down the trail.

Du Pré hobbled over to the stove, poured more tea for the two of them. Set the cups back down on the table.

Bart also had a bandage over his eye. He's learning, he is learning.

"Tell you a secret?" said Bart, raising a conspiratorial eyebrow.

"Sure," said Du Pré.

"I just up and bought a big diesel shovel. I always wanted one but I never knew how bad. So I called the big shovel dealer, said tell me about big shovels. He had an especially nice one, not too big, since I am not too big a man. Big enough, though. Pretty, too, kinda pale green. Got a stereo in the cab. Lots of levers and fun buttons. Make a new man of me."

You are doin' fine there, Bart.

"Now, I was thinking on having it racing striped but I decided that that would be in poor taste. Didn't get the fake polar bear fur upholstery either."

Hee, thought Du Pré. "Now where is this big shovel you got?"

"Well," said Bart, scratching at his cast, "I think it

might be here within the hour, maybe two, they have to move an extra power line or something."

"What?" said Du Pré.

"It was just an impulse," said Bart, "but I suddenly just had to have that pretty pale green big diesel shovel. Here. Start it up, dig a lake or something for practice."

Du Pré looked out the window.

"The ground is pretty frozen," said Du Pré.

"The salesman assured me that this here big shovel would not notice whether the ground is frozen or not."

"How big is this sucker, anyway?" said Du Pré.

"Oh, that," said Bart. "Well, they do make bigger ones, or anyway one bigger one. What I wanted, see, was those real delicate controls. You could fill a dump truck with one bite, whirl around and crack open a poached egg that was sitting on someone's head."

Du Pré considered that.

"Whose head?" he said finally.

"Uh," said Bart, pausing tastefully, "it is after all, my pretty pale green big diesel shovel. It would not do to lend it out, any more than it does to lend out one's toothbrush. Very personal item, this here big diesel shovel."

"Tell you what," said Du Pré. "When this shovel comes, I am going to put an egg on a rock, and when you crack it just so nice . . ."

"Guaranteed," said Bart.

The telephone rang. Du Pré answered it. For Bart.

Yes. Yes? Yes. Yes! Be right there.

Bart put the phone down.

"Well," he said, "it is here and we need to lead them to wherever that big shovel needs to be."

"Oh, boy," said Du Pré. He liked toys.

✤ CHAPTER 43 ✤

W ell," said Du Pré, looking up at the pale fluorescent green monster shovel, "how much you pay for this thing?"

"I got it on time," said Bart. "I paid them just the one time."

Well, all right.

Du Pré looked around at Catfoot's old claim, remembering. His father had worked here on and off for fifteen years. There was the little dragline, looked like a damn kid's toy next to Bart's big kid's toy. Little D2 cat, blade resting on the ground, a couple of hydraulic lines broken off. Rusting drums that Catfoot had filled with what he hoped was paydirt to wash down and never got to. A homemade grizzly rocker. The gold got caught in an old piece of carpet, and when all the paydirt was run, Catfoot burned the carpet and little globs of gold were left in the big old frying pan. Some smelter. Not a lot of gold, ever, but it kept Catfoot busy, and when the price of gold was left float he made out pretty good.

Du Pré remembered his days here. The old equipment was broken more often than not, his father would be cursing it in Coyote French while he banged the offending parts with wrenches.

What the West was built with, blasphemy.

Booger Tom, there, when he lost his temper and cussed with a serious heart he revealed himself to be a poet.

"Wanna come up and look in the cab of Popsicle, here?" said Bart.

"Popsicle?" said Du Pré.

"Sure," said Bart. "Don't she look like the color of those awful popsicles you used to eat when you were a kid?"

Du Pré nodded. Yes, it did.

Over time, Catfoot had moved a lot of gravels. Down thirty feet to bedrock, old pumps straining, sometimes the old man had to pawn his guns to buy diesel to keep everything going. Du Pré looked down into the deep wide hole, water in it. The dragline bucket was down there, out of sight.

When Catfoot had got down to the bedrock, he would climb down in the hole and shovel the blue-gray paydirt into fifty-five-gallon drums, haul them up with the bucket.

Red River.

Maybe a quarter-mile of dredge spoil here, years and years of work for Catfoot. Du Pré tried to remember where things were what year. He couldn't. Had the old man started at the other end and just worked steady over here? Or had he jumped around? Being Catfoot, he would have jumped around. Shit.

"Du Pré, damn it," said Bart, "this is the only time you get to set foot in my pretty cab. Got a virgin on the dash. Hairy dice on the rearview mirror. Cassette recorder and player with monster ju-ju and bunga-bunga. This thing is pretty noisy. The speakers are three feet across."

Du Pré scrambled up into the cab. He felt some stitches in his belly tear. Well, god damn them, I got work to do.

Bart turned the key, let the headring heat till the light went off. Pressed the starter. The huge engine caught and rumbled, the cab shook. Sounded very businesslike.

Bart shoved a tape in the tape machine. Tammy Wynette.

Bart fiddled with a couple levers. The huge arm extended itself, and he fiddled with some others and the bucket waggled.

Bart pivoted the cab, the arm, the bucket. The controls were light and easy. He waggled the bucket in time to the music.

"I'm gonna pick up a couple of those old drums there," he yelled, pointing with the bucket at a few rusting fifty-fives.

Something went wrong. He smashed them flat. The bucket went three feet into the frozen gravels.

"Popsicle, you whore!" yelled Bart.

"That egg, now," said Du Pré.

"What fucking egg?" yelled Bart.

"This egg," said Du Pré, removing one from his coat pocket.

They were yelling. Bart motioned for him to pay attention, he scrabbled around in the jockey box, came up with a little radio had an earplug hanging out of it and a slender microphone with a headset. The microphone was a long thin tube of clear plastic with a thin wire in it.

Du Pré put it on. He adjusted the headset. Switched on the little radio.

"Earth to Du Pré," said Bart, softly.

Damn easy to hear, this, through the earplug.

"OK," said Du Pré. "You practice with old Popsicle here and I go out and walk around, see what I can remember."

"Do my best," said Bart. "Put that egg over there on top of that post, will you?"

"Oh, hell," said Du Pré. "You can't see a damn thing for that bucket, it is half the size of my house."

"Not true, my friend," said Bart, "I went first class. This sucker has a TV camera out there." He pointed to a little screen, pressed a button. The screen came on.

"Jesus," said Du Pré, "it is not even in color. How you going to enjoy watching my blood spurt all over it if it isn't a color camera?"

"Oh, ye of little faith," said Bart.

"Oh, me of no fucking faith at all," said Du Pré. "I go put that egg on the post now."

Bart nodded.

"Du Pré," said Bart, "we are looking for a Mercury, Colorado plates, been down there a long time, right."

Du Pré nodded.

"When we find it," Bart went on, "we got a couple Masses to pay for, go to."

Du Pré nodded.

"We both go to both of them," said Bart.

"Oh, yes," said Du Pré.

♣ CHAPTER 44 ♣

Du Pré and Bart Fascelli stood by the bucket, looking at the torn metal. Some pale green paint on it. A bumper. A smashed Colorado license plate on it, all the enamel gone. The numbers were in stamped red rust, the plate was bent in half.

They looked down into the water rising in the blackish gravels.

"Well," said Bart. "There it is. You were right."

Du Pré nodded. It gave him no pleasure.

"I'll get a chain around the car," said Du Pré. "The chassis should hold, I think."

He scrambled down the pit walls, gravels loosening under his feet, water percolating everywhere. The heavy chain on his shoulder fouled his balance and he fell and came up wet and freezing. Little determined snowflakes fell from a black sky. Maybe rain, then ice. The time of the bad cold was coming. It was up there north, crouched, dark, merciless.

The time of white owls, boiling hooves for soup, leaving the frozen winter dead in the trees.

Du Pré shivered.

He ran the chain around the frame of the car, bent from the years spent under the tons of shifting gravels. These stones were headed for the Gulf of Mexico. They flowed very slowly, but they did.

The mountains stand up to their waists in their own flesh, thought Du Pré, spalled off by ice and time.

Bart moved the bucket down slowly, to where Du Pré could put the chain through one of the eyes on the lip.

Du Pré fought his way back up. He raised his hand, palm up.

Lift lift lift he motioned.

The chain lost its slack. A couple of pebbles stirred near the buried car. The frame bent a little. And then the car came up, sheet metal tearing, stones clattering down. Smashed to a dented tangled mass a fourth the size it once was.

Bart lifted it up and swung it round, set it down on the spoil drift. Water ran out of the wreck.

He killed the engine of the big diesel shovel, opened the cab door and dropped down the ladder.

Four weeks we been doing this, thought Du Pré. He looked back at the gravels they had so carefully moved, knowing what was down there, wanting to find it and not wanting to find it but having to find it all the same.

And, well, boys, there you have it.

"Not much of a Grail," said Bart.

"Have to do for the likes of us," said Du Pré. Now we can let the sad past sleep, and be maimed by it forever.

Muddy water dripped out of the wreck. A few shreds of upholstery gone mud-colored, gobs of muck stuck out of the car. The glass was all long ground to powder.

They took a spud bar and tried to pry the wreck apart. No good. Bart went back up into the cab of the shovel and fired it up again, lifted the wreck and lumbered back to the old dragline. The weight of the dead machine was enough. Du Pré chained the old Mercury to the old dragline and Bart pulled the wreck apart.

They sorted through the wreck, ran hoses on the parts. No emeralds and gold, no money, nothing.

"And no fucking map to the Lost Bullfrog Mine," said Du Pré.

Not that it mattered.

A car horn sounded. Madelaine and Maria, worried, had come out to see if Du Pré and Bart had killed themselves yet.

They brought sandwiches and hot coffee. It was mostly dark now and soon to be dark all the rest of the way.

"We have to report this," said Du Pré. "Just as soon as we god damned well feel like it."

Bart was eating a sandwich. "Sometimes after I have busted hump all day I feel like I have never tasted food before," he said. "Good sandwich."

"Come to supper tomorrow," said Maria to Bart.

Bart nodded. "Guy could do worse than be a shovel man," he said. "I have."

Du Pré, Madelaine, and Maria left then, leaving Bart to his Popsicle, thoughts, and prayers.

At the house, Du Pré drank some whiskey, didn't say much.

"You find everything that you are looking for maybe you can go back to being Du Pré now," said Madelaine, going out the door to her children. "You maybe want I leave my address with you, describe the house?"

Du Pré laughed. Madelaine, she wasn't laughing.

"See you tomorrow," said Du Pré to Maria.

He drove behind Madelaine to her home.

✤ CHAPTER 45 ✤

Du Pré drove through a strong May blizzard out to his house, wondered if this heavy snow would crush the old shed he had been meaning to shore up for the last ten years or so. He only remembered it when he couldn't do it, like the leak in the roof.

Maria was in the kitchen, baking bread. The table was piled with books and there was a new computer, too, one Bart said he could not possibly use because he was just a simple shovel operator. The computer still had the warranty card on it.

"Papa," said Maria, "there is something funny hanging in the tree back there." She leaned over the sink and pointed out the window to the willow by the little creek.

Du Pré squinted. Something white, had a couple birds on it.

"Looks like a piece of suet," said Du Pré.

"Well," said Maria, "I didn't hang it up there, pretty high."

A good eight feet off the ground. There was a path through the snow to it, from the yard, the trail went out across the white field beyond the creek.

"That's funny," said Du Pré.

The suet was hung over the stobs of the lilac Catfoot du Pré and his young bride had planted so long ago. The lilac had died, the leaves had turned yellow a couple of years ago. Du Pré had cut the dead trunks away and he had meant to grub up the roots but he had forgotten to do that.

Like hell, I hate digging up roots.

Du Pré looked down at the tracks in the snow. Coyote. The animal had stood beneath the suet, tried to leap up and get it and couldn't. When the birds pecked the slab of fat some chunks broke off and fell down into the snow. The coyote had scratched around a lot, for the good fat after this hard winter.

"OK," said Du Pré, "you old fucker."

He went to the shed, got a spud bar and a shovel. The ground was thawed, it always did under the snow. He slammed the spud into the earth, grabbed the shovel, and down about a foot and a half he hit something hard but not like a rock is hard.

Little brass box, size of a Bible.

All green, been here a while, thought Du Pré.

He took it to the house, put it in the sink and washed the dirt off. A little box, well-brazed seams all around. Du Pré looked at the bead.

Catfoot's bead, that, as much his as his handwriting.

"What you got there?" said Maria.

"Something I think belongs to Bart," said Du Pré.

He went back out to the shed, got a cold chisel and a hammer. Cut the top off the box on the kitchen floor.

Nice and dry in the box. Catfoot lay up good tight bead, there.

A suede envelope, black. A flat packet wrapped in foil. Du Pré pulled them both out. Nothing else.

"See this, now," said Du Pré to Maria. He opened the suede envelope. He lifted out the necklace, green gems and gold, all brilliant in the light.

"Oooohhhh," said Maria. She reached for the necklace. Du Pré let her have it.

Du Pré peeled back the foil. Thick packet of hundred-dollar bills.

"What's this?" said Maria. "What is all this?"

Du Pré told her all of it.

She sat at the table, looking out the window, at the failing light.

Du Pré reached across the table, took her hand, squeezed it.

"I got to go up to Bart's a minute," he said. "Talk to him about a couple Masses."

✤ C H A P T E R   4 6 ✤

Bart looked at the money and the brilliant necklace. His whole face twitched.

"What a bunch of shit," he said. "My family. A bunch of money and a bunch of shit. We hated each other. I loved Gianni. You know why? He was gone before I was old enough to know him. He must have been a prize asshole. Oh, God. I spent all my time waiting for Gianni to come back. At least he was my goddamned brother."

Du Pré rubbed his eyes.

Bart sipped his tea. He wanted a drink, bad.

"I didn't want to know, either," said Du Pré.

Bart poked the necklace like it was a prize snake that had died just to be rude.

Bart took a pouch of cheap tobacco out of his bathrobe and rolled a cigarette. He lit it. He sucked the smoke in hard and blew it out. He shook his head again.

"You people," he said.

Du Pré looked up. What?

Bart began to cry, softly.

"Us?" said Du Pré. He didn't know what us Bart meant.

"I spent all of my time whining," said Bart. "Well, boys, there you have it."

Du Pré didn't know what the fuck Bart was talking about.

Bart wailed. It was the cry of some creature wounded to death and the killers closing.

"I can't stand this," said Bart.

I can't either, thought Du Pré. So get drunk.

Bart went to the cupboard and took out the whiskey and had a lake of it.

"You people," he said again.

"What goddamned people?" said Du Pré. "You tell me that. My father killed Gianni. Well, you stupid asshole, I would have too."

Bart nodded.

"He needed killing," said Du Pré.

Bart sat back down, calm. He poked the necklace again.

"What did Gianni do to make Catfoot so mad?" said Bart.

Du Pré lit a cigarette.

"Pauline asked him to kill Gianni," said Du Pré, "and Gianni was some asshole, so Catfoot just killed him. Catfoot was a careful guy, you know, it's hard to find a body you take care. So I think he just did it."

"You people," said Bart.

"I don't know what *you people* means," said Du Pré.

"You're killers."

"Oh," said Du Pré. That.

Bart sat back hard in his chair and looked at the ceiling.

"Festerfuck," he said.

Du Pré sat and rubbed his mustache.

"Hey," he said, "what about these Masses."

"We need 'em for our souls," said Bart.

Du Pré waited. He yawned.

"How the hell could Catfoot just kill my brother and bury him and go on with his life?" said Bart.

"I got to go home," said Du Pré.

"Answer me, goddamnit," said Bart. He was starting to cry again.

"Your brother was a piece of shit," said Du Pré, "and your brother was a bad man to one of Catfoot's women. Catfoot didn't even know you lived, but he would have killed you too, he was so tired of Pauline's goddamned bitching. You don't push people so far, you know."

"You people," said Bart, again. He started another cigarette.

"My father a murderer and your brother needed killing and I am very tired of this," said Du Pré.

"I want to give this necklace to Maria," said Bart.

"She's down at the church," said Du Pré, "so we can go now."

He walked out. He whistled "Baptiste's Lament."

Many stars above.

154